To every person who has ever sat across from me and trusted me with their story.

This book exists because of your courage, your honesty, and your choice to face the difficult moments.

Thank you for allowing me to witness your pain, your laughter, your silence, and your healing.

You have shown me more about being human than any training or book ever could.

This is for you, and for every part of you that once wondered if anyone would truly listen.

"Out of your vulnerabilities will come your strength."

Sigmund Freud

Contents

Acknowledgments

This book exists because of the people who entrusted me with their stories. To my clients, past and present, I offer my deepest thanks. You invited me into the most private corners of your lives, and through your courage, honesty, and resilience, you have shaped me as both a therapist and a person. Your identities remain protected, yet your voices resonate through these pages, and I am grateful for the privilege of witnessing your journeys.

To my teachers, whose guidance carried me through the early years of training, thank you for encouraging me to think more deeply, to listen more closely, and to remember always the human being beyond the theory.

To my supervisors, past and present, Hayley Marshall and Sally Evans, I owe particular gratitude. You steadied me in moments of doubt, drew attention to my blind spots, and showed me how to remain compassionate while holding clear boundaries. This book would not have taken shape without your example and encouragement.

To those who helped bring this manuscript into being — my editor, Mick Flaherty, along with my friend, Colin McPoland; thank you for reading drafts, offering reflections, and urging me forward when the process felt heavy. Your keen eyes and patient hearts made this possible.

Finally, to those in my personal life who stood quietly beside me as I wrestled with these stories, thank you for your love, your patience, and your faith that this work was worth completing.

This is not my book alone. It also belongs to all of you.

Introduction

I feel privileged to have met so many people who have trusted me with their stories. The accounts in this book are inspired by those encounters, as well as moments from my own life. Confidentiality remains central to my work, so the people you will meet here are fictional constructs, shaped from combinations of experiences and personal reflection. They are not individuals, but characters created to reflect the struggles, questions, and hopes that many of us recognise. They could be you, a neighbour, a colleague, a partner, or a family member.

When I first became interested in psychology in 2003, I searched for books that described what really happened behind the closed door of the therapy room. At that time, Irvin Yalom was one of the few to offer glimpses into his sessions. During training, we studied theory, frameworks, and techniques; we practised with each other; and we undertook our own therapy, which remains one of the most valuable forms of learning. Still, there was a mystery about what unfolded in the quiet of a real session. In recent years, more therapists have begun to write openly, and this has helped to challenge the myth of the flawless practitioner. Books such as *The Skeleton Cupboard* by Tanya Byron, *How Does That Make You Feel* by Joshua Fletcher, and *Couch Fiction* by Philippa Perry reveal the vulnerability, doubt, and struggle that lie behind the professional façade of 'holding the space'.

I came to psychology later in life, in my thirties. For a long time, I believed I was not clever enough to study something so demanding. It felt out of reach. Then, during a personal crisis and through beginning my own therapy, I wanted to understand why I could appear successful in my professional life yet feel such failure in my personal one. It was as though two separate selves were at work, with no bridge between them. That contradiction was the beginning of my path into psychology.

Writing has since become another form of therapy. Putting these stories on paper is my way of honouring the people who have shaped my understanding of resilience, struggle, and what it means to be human. They have taught me lessons that no training manual ever could.

Most of this book is written in the third person, referring to the therapist as 'she'. At times, I move into the first person to bring in my own feelings and reflections. This is deliberate. Even though these accounts are fictional, they draw on real encounters that have challenged me, moved me, and stayed with me.

I

James

1

The Garage

'Observation precedes technique,' Eric Berne once said, and that was what we were taught. It makes sense. Meeting someone where they are begins with noticing — both them and ourselves. What are the first impressions? What draws the eye? What feeling stirs in the room? After a first meeting I make notes not only on what is said but also on posture, gaze, gesture, and what rises in me as I sit opposite them.

James was in his late fifties, married with two children, grandchildren, and a dog he adored. He had spent years working in a factory, a strong and capable man, proud of his trade. His jacket and cap marked him as a Liverpool supporter. His skin looked dry and blotched, which made me wonder briefly about alcohol, a quiet note to myself. Yet it was his eyes I remember most. They carried the weight of someone who had misplaced hope.

It was raining the first day James came to the garage, though in truth he had been brought there. He had imagined a therapy room as soft and ordered: tissues on a low table, warm lighting, perhaps a framed quote with words of encouragement. Instead he found bare concrete, a faint smell of tools, a ladder hanging on the wall behind me. In 2020, this was how it had to be. The garage allowed for social distancing during the COVID pandemic. With the door wide open to the rain, it still felt more human than another Zoom call. I gestured to the chair I'd already disinfected.

'Please, take a seat.'

He sat, unsure what came next. In coaching we called it a chemistry session. In therapy the language shifts: first consultation, initial meeting. Whatever the term, it felt to him more like sitting an exam without knowing the subject. His mouth was dry, his stomach knotted. For years he had worked in a factory filled with glass, heat, and noise. Now his hands shook when he boiled a kettle. Sleep was broken by nightmares and the shadow of shame that followed him into the day.

What struck him first was my calm. I did not rush or fill the silence. At first this unsettled him, then slowly it did not. He noticed my eyes; they met his and held steady, as though looking beyond the fog he carried.

'My name's James,' he said, his voice rough.

'Hi James.'

He waited for a question, but none came. Only quiet.

'I've never done this before.'

'That's okay.'

'My GP said it might help. There was a waiting list. So... here I am.'

'Welcome.'

That word nearly undid him. When had he last felt welcomed?

He did not speak of the nightmares, not then. He did not

speak of waking soaked in sweat, heart racing with the certainty that he had done something terrible. He did mention drinking, brushed off lightly. A beer, sometimes a bottle. He made it sound casual. I knew it was not.

His wife had urged him to try. She saw her own therapist and had said it might be good to talk. But talking was dangerous. Talking risked releasing what he had worked so hard to contain.

'I don't want to talk about… you know. Certain things,' he said, lowering his voice.

'You don't have to.'

He looked up. I was not shocked, and I was not pushing.

'Will you make me?'

'No. You decide. We go at your pace.'

Something inside him shifted. Not gone, not healed, but awake enough to listen.

The garage was cold, but it became something else. A place marked on his map, a place to meet himself. I always plugged in a small heater before he arrived. The chair was always disinfected. In those first sessions he spoke only of work, of aching knees, of poor sleep. He never said why.

One day he glanced at the ladder behind me. Just an old ladder, but something in it caught him. Mid-sentence he nodded at it.

'That's me,' he said. 'Climbing that.'

I turned. 'How far up are you today?'

He thought. 'Third rung.'

'Good to know.'

And from then on, the ladder gave us a language.

2

The Child and the Gears

James could not explain why he kept returning. He joked that it was to avoid wasting money, but even he knew that was not the truth. Something quieter drew him back each week.

By the fifth or sixth session the garage felt less strange. The chair was always there, disinfected and ready. The ladder still leaned against the wall, unchanged yet heavy with meaning. He had begun rating his days by its rungs.

'Fourth rung this week,' he said once.

She did not praise or interpret. She simply nodded. 'What helped you climb?'

He shrugged. 'The dog, maybe. A bit of quiet. No drama.'

They sat together in a silence that felt safe rather than empty. He broke it. 'You ever feel… full up? As if your head's a mess of wires, alarms, signals all going at once? Similar to spaghetti junction?'

She gave a small smile. 'Yes. That sounds overwhelming.'

'It is.'

He told her how the noise at work grated on him now, how

sudden shouts made him flinch. Break times had become unbearable; he pretended to be busy so he could avoid small talk. He did not say the word panic, not yet. He did not call it trauma. That would come later.

One morning she asked, 'If your mind is like spaghetti junction, what's your body like?'

He frowned. 'My body?'

'Yes.'

He thought. 'Similar to a car stuck in sixth gear.'

'Always racing?'

'Yeah. No brakes. Just go, go, go. Until it crashes. Or overheats. Or something blows.'

She held the moment. 'That sounds exhausting.'

'It is.'

That night he dreamed again. A corridor stretched out ahead, doors slamming behind him as he ran. He was late. Someone was screaming, though he did not know who. He never reached the end.

He told her the following session, though not all of it. Just enough. 'I think I'm broken,' he said flatly.

'No,' she replied. 'You're responding.'

'To what?'

'To everything you've survived.'

He turned his gaze away.

She waited, then asked quietly, 'Do you remember feeling safe when you were young?'

James blinked. Inside, something folded itself into shadow.

'No.'

After that, he spoke more often of the gears. The metaphor made it easier, less exposing. He could say 'I'm in fifth gear' instead of 'I'm spiralling'. He could say 'I tried to downshift' instead of 'I tried not to drink'. One day he said softly, 'I think… part of me got stuck.'

She gave him time. 'What part?'

He struggled to find words. 'A kid. A little version of me. Locked up somewhere.'

She remained silent.

'He's scared. Always watching, waiting for someone to shout, waiting for something worse.' The silence held them both.

'That makes sense,' she said gently.

He nodded, throat tight. He swallowed hard, the way he always had. By then he trusted her. Not completely, but enough. He listened when she explained that trauma does not always live in memory but in the body itself, that the nervous system can carry a crash without a single bruise. He understood that, as a man who had spent his life with tools and machines. She reminded him that the garage was his space, that he did not have to tell her everything, that some truths could wait. So he kept his grandfather to himself. Not yet. But something inside him shifted that day, as though one of the wires in his junction had loosened. On his way out he paused by the ladder.

'Maybe I'm not climbing,' he said. 'Maybe I'm just holding on.'

She smiled. 'Sometimes holding on is the work.'

3

Spaghetti Junction

The cold did not bother him anymore.

By now, James had a routine. Dog walk, coffee, then the garage. The same chair, the same heater, the same faint smell of wood and old metal. The sameness was a comfort. Everything else in his life still felt unpredictable, but the garage did not change.

Today, he sat down with a sigh that came from somewhere deep.

'Fifth rung,' he said.

She looked up. 'That's steady progress.'

'Yeah. But I'm not sure I'm going anywhere.' He paused. 'It's like I'm climbing the same rung over and over again.'

She waited.

'Spaghetti junction again. I wake up thinking about ten things I haven't done. I get anxious about work, about my grandkids, about saying the wrong thing, being the wrong thing. Then I feel like a failure for even feeling that way.'

'And what do you do when that feeling hits?'

'Used to drink. Now I go for a walk, or fix something in the shed. Or... I just sit. I try to remember what you said about gears. That I don't always need to be in six.'

She nodded. 'Do you still think of the car metaphor?'

'All the time. It helps. Makes it feel less... mad. Less like I'm going under.'

There was a time he would never have spoken those words aloud. But now he could say 'I'm struggling' without shame swallowing them back. He still could not say abuse, not yet. But he had begun to refer to 'what happened', a phrase that carried weight in the silence that followed it. She knew what he meant, even if the words were not spoken.

One session he arrived looking tired, raw.

'I dreamt I was in a courtroom,' he said.

She waited.

'I was on trial. But I didn't know what I'd done. Everyone was staring at me. Even my own son.'

'That sounds terrifying.'

He nodded. 'It was.'

She leaned forward slightly. 'Do you feel judged often?'

He hesitated. 'Only all the time.'

He spoke more about work. How his chest tightened when his supervisor walked in. How he overdid everything, covering other people's shifts, never complaining, always smiling.

'I feel like if I drop one ball, it'll all fall apart.'

She nodded. 'What happens if you do drop a ball?'

He blinked. 'I... don't know.'

'What would the little boy inside you say?'

James looked down. 'He'd say: "We're in trouble."'

Later that session, she asked quietly, 'When did you learn to be so afraid of making mistakes?'

He looked at the ladder. 'Before I even knew I was learning.'

They sat in silence. The heater clicked once, then whirred again.

'You know,' she said, 'the brain learns survival. But the body holds the score.'

James looked at her. 'That's what it feels like. Like my body's still in the past.'

'You're starting to notice that.'

He nodded.

'It's the first step. Awareness always comes before change.'

After the session he lingered by the ladder. She stayed silent.

He placed his hand on the second rung, briefly, as if in greeting.

'You know,' he said, 'this thing used to mean how far I was climbing.'

She tilted her head.

'Now I think it's more about what I'm carrying as I climb.'

The rain was soft that day. It ran down the garage window in silver lines, akin to veins. James watched it for a moment before sitting down.

He did not say what rung he was on. He did not speak for a while.

She did not fill the silence. She never did.

Eventually, he said, 'I think I want to say something today. But I'm scared of hearing myself say it.'

She paused. 'That makes sense. I am here and we can hold it together if we need to.'

He closed his eyes. 'I feel like I've been holding this in so long, it's shaped my spine. Bent me around it.'

Silence again. And then, quietly:

'It was my grandfather.'

She waited.

His voice dropped. 'He hurt me. I was a kid. I didn't understand it then, but now I know. What he did was abuse.'

The words were jagged. They did not flow. He did not describe everything, and he did not need to. The shape of the pain was enough.

She did not recoil. She stayed present. Grounded.

He spoke in fragments.

'Family knew… they didn't say anything.'

'I loved him. That's the worst part.'

'I thought it was my fault.'

She offered no platitudes, no quick answers. Only space, witness, and warmth.

'You were a child,' she said softly. 'There is no fault in that.'

Secrets weigh heavily. After that session something shifted. Not suddenly, but the air around him felt looser, as though he had exhaled a breath he had been holding for decades.

The next week he brought a folded piece of paper.

'I've been writing,' he said.

She nodded. 'Would you like to share it?'

He hesitated, then unfolded the page. His voice was steady but raw.

Hello Grandad,

We need to have a chat about what happened with you when I was a young boy...

She listened, hands still in her lap. No interruptions.

I have carried the guilt and self-blame for what happened; however, this was not my burden to carry, but yours...

His voice cracked once. Just once. He kept reading.

You have no control over me now. I am loved and valued. I am reclaiming my life and living it in accordance with my values...

He folded the letter again.

'He'll be proud of you,' she said.

'Who?'

'That boy. The one who didn't have a voice back then.'

James looked down and swallowed hard.

'I took it to the cemetery,' he said quietly. 'Read it out loud.'

She nodded, as though bowing to something sacred.

'It felt like… freedom,' he said.

The next session he brought something else: a small jar*.

'What's that for?' she asked.

He smiled. 'One of the jars.'

'Psychological hunger?'

He nodded. 'This one's for recognition.'

'What's inside?'

'A note from my granddaughter. Says "you're the best Grandad ever".'

He tapped the jar. 'Proof.'

That day, as he left the garage, he looked again at the ladder.

'I'm not counting rungs anymore,' he said.

'Oh?'

'I'm just climbing. Slowly. And I've put the letter at the bottom. It's not following me anymore.'

**In a previous session she had explained the idea of Psychological Hungers, using the metaphor of jars that can be filled in healthy or unhealthy ways. When these jars are filled in healthy ways, we feel grounded. The hungers include stimulus, recognition, contact, structure, sexual, and incident (Mardula, 2021).*

4

Gear One

He came in humming. It was not a tune exactly, more a low murmur under his breath, something he had not noticed until he caught her smile. He stopped, embarrassed.

'Sorry.'

'Don't be. You sound lighter today.'

James scratched the back of his neck. 'Yeah… bit weird, innit?'

'Not weird at all,' she said.

He settled into the chair and exhaled.

'I slowed down this week.'

She raised an eyebrow. 'Intentionally?'

He nodded. 'Took a day off work, didn't fix anything, didn't clean the shed. Just sat in the garden and listened to the birds. Had a brew… and fell asleep in the sun.'

He looked at her as if he had confessed a crime.

'I felt guilty,' he said.

'Why?'

'I kept hearing this voice saying, "You're lazy. You've wasted the day. You should be doing something."'

'And what did you say back?'

He smiled slowly. 'I said, "No. I'm in gear one."'

I felt a quiet pride rise in me. If he had been a friend, I would have reached out and hugged him. But he was not, so I simply made my mental notes.

Weeks earlier they had spoken about his relentless pace, the way he lived as though stuck in sixth gear, rushing, doing, performing. Rest had always felt unsafe. Stillness had once meant danger.

'You used to feel safest when over-functioning,' she reminded him.

He nodded. 'Yeah. I didn't feel like me otherwise.'

'And now?'

'I'm learning to like gear one.'

She handed him a small printed card with a few sentences on it.

Instead of saying, "I did nothing today," you might say:

I chose rest. I listened to my body. I recharged. I nourished myself. I allowed quiet. I made space for joy.

He read it once. Then again.

'This feels… rebellious,' he said, half-smiling.

'It's permission,' she said. 'For being, not just doing.'

He told her about a moment with his granddaughter.

'She asked if I could play shops with her. I almost said, "Not now." But I stopped myself. Sat on the floor, let her sell me bananas and fairy cakes for an hour. You should've seen her face.'

She studied him. 'And yours?'

He blinked. 'Probably softer than it's been in years.'

Near the end of the session, his face grew thoughtful.

'Rest used to feel like failure,' he said. 'Like I was falling behind.

Or letting someone down.'

'And now?'

He paused.

'Now, sometimes it feels like love.'

As he stood to leave, his gaze fell on the ladder behind her.

'I used to think it was about climbing out of something,' he said. 'But maybe it's also about climbing into myself.'

She did not answer. She did not need to.

He stepped outside, the sun warm on his face, a man learning to take up space in a life that had once felt too dangerous to live in.

5

The Jars

He brought in five jars. Real ones, glass, clinking in a small cardboard box. Clean, with neat handwritten labels: Recognition, Contact, Structure, Stimulus, Incident.

He set them carefully on the floor beside the chair.

'I've been thinking,' James said, 'about all the ways I'm full now.'

She tilted her head, smiling. 'Full?'

'Yeah. You remember those sessions when I was just surviving? Spaghetti junction, stuck in sixth, no idea what I needed?'

'I do.'

'Well, I started noticing. What fills me up... properly fills me up.'

He picked up one jar. Recognition.

'My son said he was proud of me. Unprompted. Just said it over tea. That went in this jar.'

Then Contact.

'My youngest granddaughter fell asleep on my lap last weekend. She was still holding my finger.'

Then Structure.

'I've got a rhythm now. Mondays are shed days. Fridays I pick the girls up from school. Sundays I cook. I like the shape of it all.'

Then Stimulus.

'I've got an allotment now. Never thought I'd enjoy planting spuds, but there you go.'

And finally, Incident. He laughed.

'Date night. Me and the wife went bowling. I was bloody awful. But we laughed so much. Real belly laughs.'

She watched him, gently moved.

'You've been building a life,' she said. 'One jar at a time.'

He nodded. 'That's it. The old stuff still shows up sometimes. The panic, the guilt, the dreams. But they don't take over anymore.'

'And what about the ladder?'

He turned to look at it.

'Still there. But I don't need to measure myself by it every week.'

He paused.

'You know what I think now? Healing isn't about climbing up and away from who I was. It's about coming down, back into myself. Finding the boy and letting him have space.'

Later, he told her a story.

'We were walking home from the park. My eldest granddaughter asked me, "Grandad, what do you do when you're scared?"'

He smiled.

'And for once, I didn't panic. I said, "I talk about it. I talk to someone who listens. And that helps."'

She nodded slowly. 'You're teaching her what you never had.'

'Yeah,' he said softly. 'I am.'

Before he left, he placed the Recognition jar gently on her side table.

'I want you to have this one.'

She blinked. 'Are you sure?'

He smiled. 'Yeah. You were the first one who saw me properly. Thought you should know.'

6

Reclamation

He did not bring anything to the session that day. No jars. No metaphors. No dreams to dissect. Just himself. She noticed it as soon as he walked in: the way he moved with ease, how his shoulders no longer hunched automatically, how his eyes met hers without darting away. He looked like a man who had arrived somewhere important.

'I went back to the cemetery,' he said, settling in.

She waited.

'No letter this time. No performance. I didn't even plan to speak.'

'What happened?'

He took a long breath. 'I just stood there. No script. No words. Just me. And I realised I wasn't angry anymore. Not even sad.'

Silence wrapped around them like soft fabric.

'I think I've taken everything back,' he said quietly. 'My voice. My worth. My peace. He doesn't get to keep any of it now.'

They sat with that.

Eventually, she asked, 'What does life feel like now?'

James looked out the small window at the ivy curling up the frame.

'Like it's mine,' he said.

He turned back to her.

'It's not about forgetting, is it? Or pretending it never happened.'

'No,' she said. 'It's about making sure it doesn't define you anymore.'

He nodded. 'And I don't carry him with me. I carry that boy instead. Little James. I look after him now. And he looks after me, in his own way.'

He spoke of simple things. Early mornings with his wife, toast on the radiator, his dog at his feet. The way he now paused before reacting, instead of letting fear take the wheel. How his hands no longer trembled when he spoke in meetings. How he had learned to say no and mean it. How he had stopped apologising for his own softness.

'I used to think being good meant being invisible,' he said. 'Now I know it means being true.'

Before he left, she asked him something she had not before.

'What do you think happens when we finish our work together?'

He did not look worried. Not anymore.

'I think I'll still visit the ladder sometimes. But I won't need it to tell me who I am.'

He paused.

'And when I climb now, it's not to escape. It's to reach… for life… for love… for joy.'

Outside, the rain had stopped. The garage door creaked as he pulled it open. A shaft of light caught the edge of the chair.

James turned once more and smiled.

'I used to come here to survive,' he said. 'Now I come because I'm alive.' Then he stepped out into the day, shoulders back, future open.

After he left that final session, she stayed a little longer than usual. The heater had already clicked off. The garage was quiet, still, holding the echoes of all that had been spoken here.

She looked at her chair and smiled. Therapy rooms are never just rooms, she thought. They are maps. Vessels. Witnesses.

On the wall behind her, the ladder still hung. She had never touched it. Not once. It was not hers to move. She wondered what her late husband would have thought of his ladder becoming a therapy tool. The thought made her chuckle, even through the sadness, imagining him shaking his head.

At first, it had simply been part of the garage, a leftover, unnoticed. It had lost its purpose when her husband passed away. But James had seen it. Named it. Given it meaning. And in doing so, he gave it back its purpose, just as he had done with his own life.

Each rung had once measured his pain, his progress, his hope. She had watched him cling to it, climb it, challenge it, and finally choose to let it be just a ladder again.

She thought about the first time he had sat across from her, red-faced and restless, too frightened to name what he carried. And the last time, when he had walked out with quiet pride, having reclaimed his voice, his boyhood, his boundaries.

This was the work, she thought. Not fixing people. Not giving them answers. But holding the space long enough for them to find their own.

She picked up the small jar he had left behind, the one marked Recognition. Inside was the folded note from his granddaughter: *You're the best Grandad ever.*

She held it in her palm for a moment, then placed it on the shelf above her desk. A reminder, not of what she had done, but of what he had done — how courage can look like a man walking into a garage, telling the truth, and slowly learning to rest.

Outside, birdsong cut through the early evening. She switched off the light and pulled the door closed behind her.

The ladder remained on the wall, unmoved. Having found a purpose again.

II

Melanie

7

The Crowded Room

Some days the therapy room felt more crowded than it should.

There was only one sofa across from my purple chair, a soft grey one that had survived coffee spills, tears, and the long silences that grief demands. Yet when Melanie sat there – her back rigid, her hands clasped tightly in her lap; it was as though her entire family had come in with her.

Her twin brother, who walked earlier and faster. Her father, with his quiet disappointment. Her mother, whose absence was always louder than her presence. And the sister who was never coming back.

I had expected this client to be layered, but not the sheer weight of echoes. Each word she offered seemed to ricochet through generations of silence, suppression, and survival. But this was the work. We were not here to tidy up the past. We were here to sit with it, sometimes wordlessly, and wait for the faintest sign of life in the cracks.

She never called it therapy. She called it 'my hour in the room with the purple sofa'.

And so it began.

8

The Visitor Who Didn't Want to Cry

'I just need to get on with it,' she said, eyes darting towards the window on her screen. Some of our sessions were on Zoom. Even then, she dressed up for each one: hair brushed, mascara on, a deliberate attempt to hold herself together.

'Get on with what?' I asked.

'Life. Work. You know. Everything.'

She smiled tightly, as though smiling might keep her face from falling apart. Her voice was quick, almost cheerful. If not for the tremor in her fingers, you might not notice the earthquake inside her.

Melanie was in her late thirties and worked in retail for a well-known High Street name. The job was demanding. She was engaged to a man who, by her account, sounded kind. Disabled since birth with cerebral palsy, though you would hardly know it given how fiercely she pushed herself, she spoke often of her twin. Her brother, she told me immediately, had been unaffected by the car crash their mother had during pregnancy.

'He came out perfect,' she said. 'I came out… me.'

She paused, perhaps expecting me to respond. I didn't. Silence, I have learned, is often the softest invitation. I made a quiet note of her assumption. Did she lay this at the door of the accident? Did she resent her brother?

'It's not just my sister,' she continued. 'That's why I'm here, technically. But it's not just her, it's everything.'

I nodded gently. 'We can take our time.'

She swallowed. 'I don't do well with feelings.'

'That's okay. We can start wherever you feel comfortable.'

And so we did. Not with the sister who died. Not with the mother who drank, or the father who left. We began with a woman sitting upright in a chair, determined not to cry, because for her, not crying had always meant survival.

She didn't know it yet, but something had already shifted. She had shown up.

Whether on the sofa or through a screen, that was never nothing.

9

Ghosts in the Room

By the fourth session, I had stopped wondering who Melanie might bring with her and started asking which ghosts would be loudest that day. This time it was her mother. By now, it was clear that grief for her mother remained unresolved.

'I've been dreaming about her again,' she said. 'But she's always drinking. Even in the dreams. Isn't that strange?'

'It's not strange,' I said. 'It's familiar.'

Melanie's mother had died in 2007, but in truth she had been absent long before. Alcohol had replaced presence. And presence, Melanie had learned, was a luxury rather than a right.

'She used to disappear for days. We'd pretend not to notice.' Her eyes dropped. 'I think I learned early that needing someone was dangerous.'

We sat with that. Not to fix it, not to cover it, just to notice.

She spoke about her twin brother again. 'He got everything first. Words. Steps. Her love.' She said it without malice, but the wound was there — clean and sharp.

She told me how their father expected more from her, how

pain had become her normal.

'I don't even think I register it anymore. Physical or otherwise.'

'It sounds exhausting.'

'It is. But if I stop, who am I?'

That was the question. Beneath the stories and the scars, who was she when she was not performing strength? Who was she when she allowed herself to stop?

For the first time, she leaned back in the chair. The ghost of her mother receded, and for a moment it was just her. Just Melanie. And me. And the silence, thick with possibility.

As children, when we begin to make sense of the world, we learn by watching those around us — parents, carers, authority figures. This is how we form our first ideas of love, safety, and conflict. We make decisions, often without realising, and there is always a payoff, usually in the form of recognition or acceptance from those we rely on.

Transactional Analysis describes these unconscious strategies as *Drivers* (Stewart & Joines, 2012):

- Be Perfect
- Be Strong
- Try Hard
- Please (People)
- Hurry Up

They carry the name *Drivers* because they compel behaviour. We act under their pressure, often without awareness, dragging them like invisible luggage that shapes the way we relate to others.

When working with a client, I look for these patterns. What

do they do? What do they avoid? What triggers them?

With Melanie, I often observed traits of what Joines and Stewart (2002) describe as the *Playful Resister*. On the surface there is cooperation; underneath, there is quiet resistance. These clients may delay, forget, or undermine, often with humour, charm, or apparent naïvety. They avoid direct conflict, but assert autonomy indirectly — through procrastination, "forgetting", or subtle sabotage. The dynamic is usually ambivalent: dependent on authority but resentful of it at the same time. The psychological payoff might be attention, control without confrontation, or a covert sense of superiority.

Melanie often fell into power struggles framed in "either–or" terms. Her childhood had given her two strong messages: *Try Hard* and *Be Strong*. She lived as though she was always doing her best, yet felt stuck in survival mode.

The work was to help her shift that energy into her thinking, not only her doing. Some of the realisations that proved useful for her included:

- She does not have to struggle in order to survive.
- She can ask directly for what she wants and allow others to respond positively.
- She has the freedom to be different and still belong.
- Being in pain is not the same as being weak.

10

The Body Remembers

'It's my back again. Feels like someone's twisting it from the inside.'

She was restless that day, shifting in her chair, unable to settle.

We spent the session exploring her relationship with her body. Born with cerebral palsy, she had learned early that needing help meant weakness, and that slowing down meant failure. Her *Child* had survived by pretending the pain was not real. Her *Adult* self was still carrying that same script.

'So, I push through,' she said. 'Then I collapse. Then I push through again.'

'It's a cycle.'

'It's my life.'

We spoke about compassion. Not as an abstract idea, but as something she could practise. Could she imagine speaking to her body as she might to a friend?

She laughed. 'I'd never speak to anyone the way I speak to myself.'

I let the silence hold us. The body knows. It remembers every time it was ignored, overridden, or forgotten.

'I don't want to be angry at it anymore,' she whispered.

'Then maybe we start with listening.'

That day, she promised to take a break. Not because she had earned it, but because she deserved it. A small promise, yet a seismic shift. One breath closer to healing.

Insight

The words *Child* and *Adult* are capitalised here because they refer to Eric Berne's (1961) Ego States: Parent, Adult, and Child. This framework helps us understand how we embody different parts of ourselves at different times. Melanie's *Child* had learned to survive by dismissing pain. Her *Adult* had reinforced that survival strategy. Recognising this pattern was the first step towards breaking it.

11

The Funeral That Didn't Happen

'I keep thinking she'll text me.'

Melanie said it flatly, then looked up, startled by her own words. 'I know she won't. But part of me still waits.'

Grief does not follow rules. We had already established that. But today, it was wrapped in shame. Not over her sister's death, but the way others had responded to it.

'Jane didn't come either,' Melanie repeated, referring to another friend who had not shown up. 'And I said it was fine. Again. And now it's too late to be angry, isn't it?'

We paused.

'Is it too late to feel what you feel?' I asked.

She shook her head slowly.

'I wanted her there. I really did. But I thought if I asked, I'd be… I don't know, needy.'

'What would be so wrong about being needy?'

'I'm not allowed to be.'

There it was: script logic, still alive beneath the awareness. Need equalled weakness. Wanting meant risk. And disappointment was always easier if she never asked for anything to begin with.

We explored what it might have meant, as a child, to be let down. Again, and again, and again.

By the end of the session, she said something I had not heard from her before.

'I think I deserve to be shown up for.'

It was a quiet sentence.

But the ground it stood on had taken months to prepare.

12

The Racket

'I didn't say anything to her,' she confessed, her voice taut with frustration. 'I just said, "It's fine," and she believed me. Like always.'

We were talking about a friend who had not come to her sister's funeral. Melanie had not told her she wanted her there. She had hoped her friend would just know.

'I wanted her to guess,' she admitted. 'And when she didn't, I felt abandoned. Again.'

She was beginning to spot the loop: the expectation, the silence, the disappointment, the resentment.

I nodded gently. 'And what would have happened if you had said, "I really want you there"?'

She shrugged. 'I don't know. Maybe she would have come. Maybe she wouldn't. But at least it would have been out there.'

We mapped the cycle on paper, her emotional racket — a well-rehearsed performance of unmet needs.

'I don't tell people what I want... I expect them to know... I get hurt when they don't... I tell myself people don't care... and then I don't tell them what I want.'

She stared at the loop. 'That's it. That's exactly it.'

And in naming it, she began to unpick it. That day, she practised a sentence aloud:

'I need you.'

It sounded strange in her mouth. But it was hers.

13

It's OK to Be Sad

She cried today. Not a tear sneaking out while she apologised for being 'emotional', but a full, heaving sob, the kind that came from somewhere far older than the present moment.

'I miss her so much,' she said. 'And I hate that I'm still angry.'

We sat in that grief. We did not fix it. We did not reframe it. We allowed it.

I introduced Tonkin's model of grief: not shrinking the grief to fit life but growing life around the grief. She listened, wide-eyed.

'That's it,' she whispered. 'It hasn't gone. I've just... built more around it.'

She spoke of her sister, the one who died too young, too broken, too misunderstood. She spoke of addiction, of PTSD (post-traumatic stress disorder), of silence. And of love, tangled in all of it.

And then, as if in defiance of all the years she had been told to 'man up', she sat on the grey sofa and wept.

It was not breaking down. It was breaking open. And that

was the difference.

14

A Different Kind of Strength

She arrived smiling. Not the brittle, polite kind, but something looser. There was light in her voice.

'I told my boss I needed a day off, and I didn't apologise.'

I smiled back. 'How did that feel?'

'As if I'd committed a crime,' she laughed. 'But also… as if I meant it.'

Today, we spoke not of loss, but of worth.

She told me about her childhood: how, even with pain in her legs, she insisted on walking unaided. How she hid her discomfort, refused extra help, took pride in being 'the tough one'.

'My dad once said, "You're not broken, so stop acting like it." So, I spent years pretending I wasn't in pain.'

'And what did that cost you?'

She paused. 'Everything. Energy. Joy. Sanity.'

We talked about redefining strength: not as stoicism, but as honesty. Not as grit, but as permission to stop. Permission to feel, to need, and to rest.

'You're not less capable because you listen to your body,' I said. 'You're more.'

She nodded. And then, very softly: 'I don't think I need to prove anything anymore.'

Her voice cracked on 'need'. It was the most honest she had ever sounded.

15

The Day She Didn't Break Down

'I felt… happy.' She said it as though it required a disclaimer. 'It was weird. I went to the park, and it was sunny, and I wasn't in pain for once. And I just… felt good.'

I nodded. 'That sounds lovely.'

She blinked. 'It scared me.'

Melanie had been making progress, measured and deliberate, but joy was not a language she spoke fluently. Grief, guilt, pain — these she knew by heart. Happiness felt like speaking in a foreign tongue, uncertain and exposed.

'I almost ruined it,' she admitted. 'My brain went, "What's going to go wrong next?" Like it couldn't let me just have it.'

We explored what it meant to allow joy. That it was not betrayal to the ones she had lost. That her sister would not resent her for laughing. That feeling good did not mean she was done grieving.

'I'm afraid if I feel happy, it'll all come crashing down again.'

'Maybe it will,' I said gently. 'But maybe you'll know how to catch yourself now.'

She sat with that. And then, almost shyly, she said, 'I'd like to feel it again. Without apologising for it.'

It was the first time she had claimed joy. Not stumbled into it, but reached for it.

The purple chair did not just hold sorrow anymore. It held sunlight too.

16

The New Decision

'This is our last one, isn't it?' she asked.

I nodded.

She exhaled, slow and heavy. 'It feels… big. But okay.'

We revisited the beginning: the tight smiles, the trembling hands, the deep belief that needing others made her weak.

'I've learned how to say what I want,' she said. 'I'm not always good at it, but I'm trying.'

'You don't have to be perfect at it.'

She smiled. This one was not brittle at all.

We spoke of the sister she lost. Of how the grief had shaped her but no longer defined her. Of how she still had bad days, but now let others in when they came.

'I always thought I had to handle everything on my own,' she said. 'But I don't. And that's not failure. That's… human.'

The purple chair was quiet, as if it, too, knew its job was nearly done.

She stood up at the end. Not because she had all the answers, but because she now trusted herself to keep asking the questions.

'I think I'll miss this chair,' she said. 'But maybe that's okay too.'

I nodded. 'You carry it with you now.'

17

The Chair Stays

The room is still. The purple chair is empty. It is strange how quickly the absence settles in. For months, it had been her place of honesty, resistance, grief, breakthrough. Now, it simply waits.

But in the quiet, I remember her words. 'I think I'll miss this chair,' she said. 'But maybe that's okay too.'

Therapy ends, but the work continues. It shows up in morning routines, in difficult conversations, in quiet self-forgiveness. It echoes in laughter that no longer needs to be earned, in rest that no longer demands permission.

Melanie did not leave healed. Healing is not a destination. But she left aware. Equipped. Softer where she once was armoured, and stronger where she once felt broken.

Clients move on, and they stay with us too. Not in burden, but in legacy.

And the purple chair? It remains. Not to hold what is broken, but to welcome what is becoming.

Always ready. Always waiting. For whoever sits down next.

III

Paulina

18

The Ones We Lose Quietly

The therapist arrived to her supervision* session with a stillness that felt familiar, not grief exactly, but a relative of it. The kind of stillness that comes when something unresolved has taken up residence in the body.

'There's a girl I still think about,' she said.

The supervisor acknowledged, gently curious.

'Paulina... she was in her mid-twenties, Bulgarian. Brilliant. Beautiful. So fragile. She came to Manchester to study, and was working in a pub. She lived with her Italian boyfriend; he was good to her, patient. From what she told me, anyway...'

The therapist's hands were in her lap, fingers loosely linked.

'She was one of those clients who felt like a live wire, always sparking with intensity. Her thoughts ran fast, and deep, and dark. She cried easily. Obsessed easily. Loved too hard, too fast. And underneath it all was this constant ache of being far from home. I could relate to that, you know...'

She looked away for a moment, as if remembering her face.

'I saw her for a while. She was struggling with depression, obsessive thinking. There were early signs, flickers, of something more serious. But she was still functional. Still "managing". We worked on grounding. On reframing. On trying to build a fragile structure around the chaos.'

The therapist's voice grew quieter.

'And then one day, I got the call.'

A silence stretched between them. A different kind of grief.

'She'd been admitted to hospital. A psychotic episode apparently. She'd tried to attack her boyfriend with a knife.'

She looked down.

'She gave them my name. Said I was her therapist.'

The supervisor didn't interrupt.

The therapist's voice tightened.

'I never saw her again. No goodbye. No closure. Just a call, a shock, and silence.'

She looked up, eyes sharp with something unnameable.

'I checked her Facebook page weeks later. Just to see if she was alive. She was. Or at least… the profile was.'

They sat in the weight of that.

'People talk about therapy as if it's clean and structured, but sometimes it isn't. Sometimes it ends without warning. Sometimes you're left holding fear, or questions, or a thread you were never allowed to finish.'

The therapist took a deep breath.

'I worried about her for months. Still do, sometimes. Did she stay in treatment? Did she go home? Did she survive the shame?'

She looked away again.

'And what happens to that worry when you're a therapist? You can't reach out. You can't check in. And I know I wasn't supposed to check her Facebook page… You have to stay behind your professional walls while your heart stands at the window.'

She added, more softly:

'I've lost clients to distance. To silence. To shadow. But this one… this one stayed lodged in me.'

At the end of the session, she stood slower than usual.

'Grief has rituals,' she said. 'Funerals. Condolences. Stories. But this kind of loss has nothing. No container, just absence.'

She looked back.

'There are names I'll never talk of again, but I carry them. Not for what we resolved, but for what we never got the chance to.'

*Supervision in psychotherapy is not just a professional requirement; it is our lifeline. It offers a space where the therapist, so often the steady presence for others, can bring their own doubts, emotional weight, and questions without fear of judgement. In the quiet, reflective rhythm of supervision, we are reminded that we are not alone in this work. It is where we stay grounded, held, and gently challenged. Supervision nourishes our capacity to care, to see clearly, and to grow, so that we can keep showing up with courage and compassion for those who entrust us with their stories. It is also our quality-control mechanism, checking in with a skilled, more experienced therapist on what we are doing, what we are not doing, and whether our own issues have become entangled with the client's.

19

The Therapist's Grief

She sat quietly for a long time before speaking.

'There's a kind of grief we're not allowed to have,' she said finally. 'Not publicly. Not fully. It's the grief for clients.'

She let the words land.

'Not just the ones who die, though some do. But the ones who disappear. Who deteriorate. Who ghost you. Who break down in ways you can't follow. The ones you worry about at night, but have to pretend not to think of during the day.'

She glanced at the supervisor, almost apologetic.

'I know we're trained for this. Boundaries. Containment. Professional detachment. But you can't sit with someone in their pain every week and not feel it. You can't walk someone to the edge of their despair and not carry something back with you.'

She looked away.

'And then when it all falls apart, when they're admitted, or vanish, or spiral out, you're just… left. You can't call. You can't ask. You can't even say, I miss you.'

Her hands were resting gently in her lap now.

'We learn to say things like I hold you in mind. Or I'm here if you return. But that doesn't touch the ache of not knowing.'

She gave a bitter smile.

'Clients think we forget them. Some even apologise when they come back after months away. They don't know that we do remember. That sometimes we grieve them like ghosts.'

The supervisor asked quietly, 'Do you think it gets easier?'

She considered this for a few seconds.

'No,' she said. 'But I think you learn how to carry it better. You learn where to store the sorrow. Which memories to return to, and which to bless and release.'

She paused.

'And you realise that you're allowed to hurt. You're allowed to feel the cost of caring. You just have to do it in silence.'

She shared how she sometimes lit a candle for clients she lost. Not to death, but to the unknown.

'I never say their names. I'm terrible at remembering names anyway. But I remember their eyes. Their stories. Every single detail. The way they looked at me when they finally let the mask slip.'

She exhaled.

'And I let myself mourn what I'll never know.'

Toward the end of the session, she said:

'No one teaches you what to do with the unfinished work. The stories you'll never see the end of. You're just supposed to file it away. Supervision. Ethics. Closure. And in the file.'

She looked up.

'But some of them live in you.'

At the door, she stopped.

'There's a quiet cost to this work. Not just burnout. Not just tiredness. But heartbreak. Tiny, professional heartbreaks that build up like sediment.'

She smiled, softly.

'And still, we do it. Not because we're immune, but because we know that sometimes, just being there is what keeps someone tethered. Even if only for a while.'

20

The Ones Who Return

The therapist walked into the room that day with something different in her eyes, not relief exactly, but recognition. The kind that arrives when a long-held question is finally answered.

'She came back,' she said softly, her voice almost reverent.

The supervisor didn't need to ask who.

'A client I hadn't seen in almost three years. No goodbye. No closure. One day she just stopped coming. Emails bounced. Number disconnected. I assumed she'd vanished into the fog.'

She sat gently, as if she didn't want to disturb the delicate truth she was about to speak.

'And then last week... there she was. A new email. Same name. Same soft tone. Just three lines.'

She smiled, small but real.

'I'm not sure if you remember me. I'd like to come back. If it's still okay.'

'I remembered her,' she said. 'Of course I did.'

She spoke of the first session back, how tentative the client was, as though re-entering sacred ground.

'She kept saying sorry, for disappearing, for ghosting, for "failing" therapy, as she put it.'

The therapist paused.

'I told her what I always tell them: There is no failure in therapy. Only timing.'

She smiled faintly. 'I don't think she believed me. Not at first.'

She described the quiet joy of rediscovering someone.

'How you start again, but not from scratch. There's a map already drawn between you, it's just a little weathered now.'

She leaned forward.

'It's feels like finding a door in your house you forgot was there, and when you open it, you realise someone's been living there all along.'

She grew quieter, more reflective.

'These moments… they're rare. And they feel like grace.'

The supervisor nodded gently.

'Because not every story ends. Some just pause.'

She thought for a moment.

'I used to think closure was something I gave, a clean ending, a resolved narrative.'

She shook her head.

'But now I think real closure is knowing they can return, and that when they do, you meet them without judgement. Just presence.'

She spoke about other returns, brief, unexpected, healing.

'One sent me a postcard. Just said, I'm okay now. You helped more than you knew.'

She smiled again, a quiet tear threatening.

'I keep that one in a drawer.'

At the end of the session, she stood slowly.

'There's something sacred in return,' she said. 'Not just for them. For us too.'

She turned to the supervisor.

'It reminds me that the work we do doesn't vanish. Even if they leave. Even if we never hear from them again. Something stays.'

She opened the door.

'And sometimes, it finds its way back.'

IV

Helena

21

The Wall with the Broken Glass

The room was warmer now. Spring light poured in through the window, soft and pale. But Helena still felt cold. She sat, hands resting in her lap, holding the edge of an old photograph. Not one she had brought in, but one she saw in her mind.

A cement wall, topped with broken glass. Lagos, Nigeria. Childhood.

"My father left Greece with three years of school and no English," she began. "He taught himself architectural design and pidgin English. Built a company from nothing. Built a life."

She paused.

"And we lived behind walls."

The therapist nodded gently, encouraging without pressing.

"They say you only realise how unusual your childhood was when you finally compare it with someone else's. But I didn't have anyone to compare it with. I had no reference point. I thought filtering brown water, boiling it, filtering it again, was normal. I thought it was normal to never stop at red lights. To never go out at night. To never truly feel safe."

Her voice was steady, but the words carried weight.

"We had guards. We had bars. We had a pantry full of Greek food with expiry dates that lasted years. I didn't know what stability meant. I only knew what it was like to adapt."

A pause.

"To survive."

Later in the session, she spoke of the day the car was attacked. This was the 1970s, when demonstrations in Lagos were common. The 1978 "Ali Must Go" Protests, against rising student fees, were described as some of the most violent student agitations of the 1975–1979 Mohammed/Obasanjo military administration.

"I was in the van with my dad's business partner's son. We were both just kids. I was around seven, he must have been ten or eleven. And they started banging on the windows, screaming, hitting it with sticks and stones. My parents were in another car with my little brother. They got away. We didn't."

Silence filled the room.

"I thought that was it. That that would be the end. We managed to get away because our driver happened to be of the same tribe as the attackers, Yoruba."

Her voice trembled, then steadied.

"My mother and baby brother managed to get on that plane, and I didn't. I got ill. At that age I seemed to be sensitive with tonsillitis. Or was it my inability to speak up and express what I really needed?

"And then, I flew alone to Athens. Lagos, Zurich, Athens. Unaccompanied minor*. A baby still, really. And I thought it was cool at the time. Isn't that strange? The things we tell ourselves just to keep moving."

The therapist leaned in gently. "What did that teach you?"

Helena looked up. "To not need anyone. To be okay alone. To make danger look like adventure. And later in life I was proud that I was an independent woman..." she said, her tone sharp with sarcasm.

Another pause.

"And to not know where I belonged."

*The term *unaccompanied minor* struck a chord with me when I was reading Matthew Perry's autobiography (2022). Perry describes travelling at age five from Montreal to Los Angeles alone, labelled as an unaccompanied minor, to visit his father after his parents' divorce. He wrote of feeling terrified and alone during that first long-haul journey, but upon seeing the lights of Los Angeles, he felt some relief because he knew he would soon be with a parent. He reflects that the repeated experience of flying solo "taught him that he wasn't wanted," and he continued to refer to himself as an unaccompanied minor well into adulthood. A symbol of profound abandonment and emotional loneliness, or what I would call feeling like the black sheep of the family.

If it weren't for the resemblance, I might have assumed I was adopted. I know the 1970s were a different era, that things were done differently, even parenting. At the same time, I find it interesting that I thought this was the norm and I didn't mind. And it wasn't the only incident. It always surprised me later, in conversations with friends, when I realised what their parents did for them, while I thought it was "cool" to do these things alone.

22

No Identity

The therapist's question lingered from last week: "What did that teach you?"

Helena hadn't answered then. Not fully. It followed her home. It sat with her in the kitchen. It whispered through old family photographs and echoed every time she caught herself switching between languages without noticing.

So today, she came ready.

"I don't know what I am," she said as soon as she sat down. "I never have."

The therapist looked at her, not startled, just present.

"In Lagos, I was a Greek girl in a German school with Nigerian friends, speaking English with a pidgin twist. At home, we ate lentils and called it *fakes,* but I played barefoot in the compound like the German kids. I thought they were cooler than me. Freer."

Helena smiled faintly. "They were allowed to be messy. To climb trees. I wasn't. I was expected to be good. Polite. Clean."

She paused.

"I chose to stay in Lagos when my mum left with my little

brother. They asked me, Greece or Nigeria? And I said Nigeria. Because it was all I knew. But I didn't understand that what I was choosing was rootlessness. How can an eight-year-old make that decision anyway..."

The therapist waited.

"I spent most of my time with a German family. I started dreaming in German. Thinking in German. I wanted to be German. It felt like freedom."

Her voice softened.

"But I wasn't German. I wasn't Nigerian either. And when I was finally sent back to Greece... against my will."

Helena's eyes glazed slightly. She stared just beyond the therapist.

"I didn't fit. I couldn't understand the language properly. I had to sit a written exam, which I tried to fail, but it was so easy that I passed despite the mistakes I deliberately made. I wanted to be part of the German Department, but one of your parents had to be German. So I ended up in the Greek-German Department. My Greek was so bad they didn't grade me for two years."

The therapist said nothing. She didn't need to.

"I didn't just resist the language," she whispered. "I resisted the identity. I hated everything Greek because it reminded me of not belonging. I wasn't homesick. I was identity-sick."

Silence.

"I used to sit in the bathroom of our concrete apartment in Athens and cry," she continued. "I was skin and bone. I cried until I had nothing left. And nobody knew..."

The therapist's voice was gentle: "What were you grieving?"

Helena blinked. "The person I was in Lagos. The one who was allowed to be different. Who didn't stand out because everyone stood out. I didn't realise how much freedom there was in not fitting into one box."

She leaned back.

"I know now I wasn't grieving a country. I was grieving belonging."

Before leaving, Helena looked at the purple chair.

"You know what I think?" she said. "Belonging isn't about where you're from. It's about who can hold your story without trying to edit it."

The therapist nodded.

"And here," Helena said, gesturing to the space, "it's the first time I've let the story breathe."

23

The Chocolate and the Bin

Helena arrived quietly that day. There was something different about her energy, not withdrawn, exactly, but careful. Contained.

She sat, hands folded in her lap.

"I want to talk about Germany," she said.

The therapist waited.

"Not the school years. Later. When I was working there."

A long pause.

"I had everything on paper: success, seniority, international assignments. I ticked all the boxes. I was part of what Human Resources called a 'talent pool', on a fast-track development journey. Airline lounges, corporate dinners, the whole shebang."

Another pause.

"But I was dying inside."

She exhaled slowly.

"I remember walking into a supermarket at five in the afternoon, right after work. Kaufhof it was called," she said in an almost perfect German accent. "I was on autopilot. I'd pick up three or four kilos of chocolate. Nothing fancy. Just volume. Something I could disappear into."

Helena's voice was calm, almost clinical.

"I'd take it home, unwrap it all, and eat it. In silence. Ten, fifteen minutes tops. And then I'd cry. Or hate myself. Or both. Sometimes I'd throw it away. And sometimes..."

She looked at the floor, her voice dropping.

"Sometimes I'd go digging through the bin to get it back. Past kiwi peels, eggshells, tea bags, whatever else was there. Just to finish what I'd started."

The therapist didn't flinch. Just breathed with her.

"It wasn't about the chocolate," Helena added. "It was about the hole. And trying to fill it with anything that didn't ask questions."

They sat for a moment in shared quiet.

"You know what's cruel?" she said finally. "At work, I was the cheerful one. The strong one. The one who didn't get tired. No one knew I was falling apart."

The therapist paused. "And did anyone ever ask?"

"No," Helena said. "But even if they had, I wouldn't have told them. I didn't know how. I fooled everyone."

She described the numbness that came later. How the antidepressants flattened everything. How even crying felt like a memory she couldn't reach.

"I would look out of the window in my tiny apartment on Stresemann Strasse and I could understand, truly understand, why someone might want to jump."

Her voice didn't tremble. It was flat. Detached.

"I wasn't alive. I was functioning. And then one Thursday, I just couldn't get up from bed. For the first time in my life, I didn't go to work. I didn't even try."

Another pause.

"I didn't care."

The therapist leaned in slightly. "And then?"

"I flew back home for a long weekend. No one knew. I read a leaflet in my doctor's office. It said depression and binge-eating disorder. And for the first time, something clicked."

She smiled faintly.

"That's when I first started therapy. It saved my life."

At the end of the session, she looked up.

"People ask me now if I still eat chocolate."

The therapist smiled. "And do you?"

Helena laughed. "Yes. Like a normal person. Because I'm not trying to disappear anymore. I'm allowed to be here. I'm allowed to feel."

Later, she showed me her new tattoo: a phoenix across her shoulder blade. A piece of art, etched in pain and colour.

"There's something satisfying about it," she explained. "The sting of the needle, the permanence. It's like wearing the same T-shirt every day with the logo you want the world to see. Only this time, it's the truth."

The phoenix is a symbol of rebirth, transformation, and new beginnings. The core remains, but the story integrates. Darkness and light. Old wounds and new freedoms. That is therapy: not erasing the scars, but carrying them as part of a whole.

Clinical Note: Binge Eating Disorder (BED)

Binge Eating Disorder was formally recognised in the DSM-5 (Diagnostic and Statistical Manual of Mental Disorders) in 2013. While long observed, it had often been overlooked compared with anorexia or bulimia. Common signs include:

- Eating much more rapidly than normal
- Eating until uncomfortably full
- Eating large amounts when not physically hungry
- Eating alone due to embarrassment
- Feelings of guilt, disgust, or depression afterwards

BED often co-occurs with depression, anxiety, or substance misuse. Physical complications can be severe, including heart and kidney problems. While many sufferers conceal symptoms for years, BED is treatable with the right therapeutic support.

24

The Exit Plan

Helena arrived that day with something in her hand. A folded piece of paper, edges worn, creased as though it had been carried for years. She placed it gently on the side table.

"What's this?" the therapist asked softly.

"My resignation letter," Helena replied. "I've kept a copy. Not because I regret it, but because it was the moment I took my life back."

She leaned into the chair, her body relaxing in a way it hadn't before.

"I was the Human Resources Director for a couple of countries at this big corporate organisation. It sounds impressive, right? Big role. Big pressure. Big name on your CV."

A pause.

"But it came at the cost of everything else."

She looked down at her hands.

"I had climbed so fast I didn't realise I was climbing the wrong building."

"The incident I told you about in our last session… that was

2004 in Dusseldorf. I hit rock bottom. But something cracked open."

Helena smiled faintly.

"That's also when I started writing. First a case study. Then a book."

"You published your story?"

"Sort of," she said. "I disguised it as fiction. A composite case study, but it was me."

She paused.

"I think part of me hoped no one would find out. And another part hoped everyone would. I desperately wanted to be seen. Mrs Independent who had learned not to ask for help, didn't know another way."

"And what did it feel like, to tell the truth?"

Helena looked thoughtful.

"Like removing a mask so tight I'd forgotten it wasn't my skin."

She described what came next. Studying psychology; the slow shift from corporate command to human connection. Launching her own company with her own name on the door.

"People thought I was brave," she said. "I wasn't brave. I was desperate."

She smiled, but her eyes were fierce.

"Desperate to feel free again. Desperate to stop selling my time in exchange for burnout."

The therapist asked gently, "What do you do now?"

Helena paused.

"I work more than ever. But I don't work. I love what I do. I help people. I write. I speak. I hold space. I don't clock in. I don't wear masks. I don't ask permission to rest."

Before leaving, she placed the resignation letter back in her bag.

"Sometimes people wait until they break to begin again," she said. "But what if we didn't have to?"

The therapist met her gaze.

"Would you have listened, if someone had told you that before?"

Helena shook her head. "No. But I might've needed them to try anyway."

She stood, lighter than when she walked in.

"Freedom isn't just about leaving," she added, hand on the door. "It's about finally choosing."

V

Simon

25

Through The Looking Glass

"Not all who wander are lost." – Alice in Wonderland.

He had always been one of her favourite clients. A sound engineer in his mid-twenties, soft-spoken but brimming with restless intensity. He swore a lot, but she didn't mind. He often joked that his brain had too many tabs open, frequencies overlapping, distortions in perception he couldn't quite calibrate. He was functional and eccentric, not unwell, until this day.

He entered the room a little late, which wasn't unusual for him, breathless, eyes wide. Not anxious exactly, more disoriented.

"I don't know what's happening," he said. "You're… far away. Like a doll. But huge. Your face is too close. No… wait… too small. I can't tell."

The therapist sat perfectly still, her voice calm.

"You're here," she said. "You're safe. Can you tell me what else you're experiencing?"

He held his head.

"My hands are enormous. But also not mine. My voice sounds like it's underwater… or slowed down. I tried to drink tea and the cup stretched in my hand. It scared the shit out of me. Time isn't working. It's sticky… or fast."

He looked terrified and utterly lucid in his terror.

"I know this isn't real. I know something's wrong with how I'm seeing things. But it feels real. You feel like you're flickering."

The therapist recognised it, though she had never seen it play out in front of her. Alice in Wonderland Syndrome. Not whimsical, but surreal horror. A neurological condition that distorts spatial perception, time, and body image. Migraine-related, sometimes viral, sometimes stress-triggered, often accompanied by depersonalisation. A perfect storm of terror that makes the familiar grotesque.

She breathed slowly, so he would follow.

"You're having a perceptual shift," she said. "It has a name. It won't hurt you. I know it feels frightening, but it's not permanent. I'm here with you. Let's ground together."

He shook his head.

"No, I don't know where my legs are. They're either massive or they've disappeared. I feel like I'm floating outside the room. Can you… can you say my name?"

She did.

It startled him.

"That sounded… warped. Like slowed tape."

She guided him back to the body.

"Can you press your feet into the ground? Feel your heels… your toes… try to find the pressure."

He was crying now.

"Everything's melting. And my thoughts are too loud. I hear myself think before I say anything."

She stayed with him.

"Let's find something solid. Can you tell me one object you can touch right now?"

He reached for his water glass.

"It's huge… but cold… okay… it's real. My hand's shaking. But it's touching it."

"Good," she said. "Keep going. Can you tell me what colour your shirt is?"

He looked down, blinking hard.

"Grey. I think. It keeps… changing, but I know it's grey."

"Perfect," she said.

For forty minutes, she held him in that strange space, not pulling him out, not denying his experience, but anchoring him in fragments of shared reality. Noticing, naming, and slowing everything down. He began to regulate. Very slowly.

"I feel a little more here," he said, near the end.

"You are here," she replied.

He exhaled.

"I thought I was losing my mind… you didn't flinch."

"No," she said softly. "You weren't alone."

After the session, she sat in silence. This was the edge of the work. Not the diagnosis, not the label. The staying. The non-reactive witnessing of someone else's altered world, without trying to erase it.

She knew he would need more, a medical review from a neurologist. But that day, in that hour, what he needed most was not certainty. It was presence.

26

Echoes of the Unreal

He looked different this time. Less haunted, still hesitant. Someone who had come through a storm and wasn't sure the sky would stay clear.

"I feel like I should apologise," he said.

"There's nothing to apologise for."

"I just I've replayed it all. That session. What I said, what I saw. It's like remembering a bad dream, but with CCTV footage."

"That's a good metaphor," she said. "Something happened to your perception. Your brain was under a kind of pressure. And you were able to name it, even inside the chaos."

He paused. "Was it real?"

"In a way, yes. Your experience was real. The distortions, the fear, that was your reality in that moment. What matters is how we hold that experience. Together."

He studied her face.

"I keep wondering why it happened. I had migraines when I was younger. But never like that. Why now?"

She didn't answer immediately.

"Sometimes extreme stress opens a fault line in the system.

What's been kept underground starts leaking through perception itself."

He sat with that.

"I think I haven't been okay for a while. I work in sound, right? I'm always listening to outside noise. But inside, it's been chaos."

"Tell me about the chaos."

He spoke of sleepless nights and chest tightness. Of grief he hadn't named. Of being a man who helped everyone but never asked for help.

"And then in the session… when you stayed… when I thought I was losing it… something softened. You didn't try to bring me back. You stayed with me."

"That's what I do," she said. "I stay."

His eyes shone.

"Maybe that's what I needed all along."

27

The Cost of Staying

There are days when the silence after a session feels heavier than the session itself. Not because of what was said, but because of what was held.

After the sound man left, she didn't move from her chair. She simply breathed.

To stay with someone inside their altered state without flinching, without rushing, without rescuing is to become a tuning fork for fear. You vibrate with their terror, absorb their confusion, but stay grounded enough not to echo it back. It's a quiet act of sacrifice, a private bravery, and it has a cost.

She didn't often talk about this part. The physical tiredness after intense sessions. The low-grade anxiety that sometimes lingered for hours. The way her own perception occasionally blurred, reality thinning just at the edges.

There were evenings when she'd lie in bed and wonder if she'd really come back from all the places her clients had taken her.

Is this mine, or theirs?

Am I still inside the room? Or did a part of me stay behind in their grief, their panic, their unreality?

She grounded herself with rituals. Peppermint tea. Feet flat on the floor. A hard workout or yoga. The weight of her dog beside her, steady and unquestioning. Definitely the dog's presence. He was her anchor, and whether he knew it or not, he kept her tethered.

Still, there were echoes. Always echoes. Supervision became essential. Every fortnight without fail.

And yet, she chose to return, session after session. Because sometimes, not always, but sometimes, a client would say:

"You stayed."

Or:

"You didn't try to fix me. You just let me exist."

And in those moments, she knew. The staying was the work. Not interpretation. Not advice. Not treatment plans. Just presence. Being the real thing in an unreal moment.

VI

Bernard

28

Love and Hate

The psychotherapeutic relationship, though professional, is also deeply intimate. People confide in you their worst nightmares, fantasies, fears, and wishes they may never admit to themselves.

Naturally, feelings of perceived love or hate can emerge. I underline *perceived* deliberately. A therapist's genuine interest in a client's story can be interpreted as personal interest or even romantic love if that fits the client's internal map.

Dangerously generalising here, but why do clients seek therapy? Across all the differences, there is often a theme of wanting to develop or repair the capacity for intimacy and love. For some, it is about the absence of love. For others, the inability to express love toward themselves or others. Romantic love, parental love, recognition, self-acceptance, rejection, approval, loss of love, death — it is almost always somewhere in the equation.

A very tall man, with the assured posture of someone used to taking up space, came into her practice. He dressed from another era: tweed jacket, hat, waistcoat with a silver chain.

Mid-fifties, successful by his own account, unfailingly polite in the early months. A posh English accent, despite being born and bred in the Northwest. Downton Abbey style.

The early work was straightforward: professional burnout, the sense of having "lost the plot" after separation, drifting through online dating, rows with his ageing father, unprocessed grief for his mother. But around the fourth month, the tone changed.

It began with small remarks: "You look tired today, Maria, you should take better care of yourself." Framed as concern, but carrying something else. Then comments about my hair, my clothes. Then, a glancing reference to how "women are just wired differently, more emotional, less logical," delivered with a half-smile as though it were a private joke.

At first, I met these moments with curiosity, asking where such ideas came from. But the answers circled the same centre: a worldview where women were to be appraised, managed, and put in their place.

One day, he mentioned he'd been "listening to a lot of Andrew Tate lately."

Trying to manage my response, I asked what resonated with him. "Everything! I totally agree with his ideas about women!"

Andrew Tate is a British-American influencer charged with rape, human trafficking, and forming an organised crime group to exploit women. I once watched a documentary on him. Disturbing doesn't begin to cover it.

The client spoke with quiet conviction, convinced he had finally found someone telling "the truth" about men, women, and the "natural order." The air in the room shifted. My body registered before my mind did — shoulders tense, breath shortened. It wasn't simply disagreement. It was the awareness that the therapeutic alliance, the foundation of our work, was fracturing.

When he began to express feelings toward me not as his therapist but as a woman, I knew we had crossed into dangerous ground. These weren't explorations of transference. They carried entitlement, as if my role was flexible, negotiable.

I took it to supervision. My supervisor asked the questions that matter:

- Can this dynamic be worked with in the service of the therapy?
- Can you hold both your safety and your authority in the room?
- Is there a way to name the misogyny without humiliating the client?

We discussed strategies. The risk of colluding through silence. The deeper function of his beliefs, how they protected him from grief and from the unbearable idea that women might not exist for his benefit.

In the following session, I named what I was seeing. I told him there were comments and attitudes emerging that were incompatible with the respect and safety therapy requires. I invited him to reflect on them.

He listened, but his eyes hardened. "You're reading too much into things," he said. "You're letting your politics get in the way."

And I knew then the work could not continue.

Ending therapy is never easy. It is not a punishment, though it can feel like one to the client. It is the recognition that the container has cracked beyond repair.

I wrote to him, documenting our last session and the reasons for ending. I offered referrals. I kept my language professional, though the experience left its mark on me. Because boundaries are not only about protecting the therapist. They also protect the client from work already compromised.

Sometimes, the most therapeutic act is to say:

"This space can no longer hold what it is meant to hold."

And to let the door close.

29

Behind Closed Doors

The supervision room always smells faintly of bergamot tea and old books. A different kind of safety lives here; not the safety I offer my clients, but the safety where I can take my armour off.

I tell my supervisor about him. Not just the facts — the Andrew Tate references, the comments on my appearance, the air that grew heavier each week, but also my body's reaction before my mind caught up. The tightness in my chest. My voice becoming overly careful, overly professional, as though I were bracing.

She listens the way only an experienced supervisor can: without rushing to fix, without dismissing, letting the words land in the stillness between us.

We go through the clinical questions first. Could the misogyny have been worked with? Could the transference have been explored safely?

I hear myself say, "Maybe... but it would have been at my expense."

There it was. The quiet truth. To work with him would have

meant tolerating devaluation and hostility that would corrode my capacity to hold him with empathy.

Then we moved into the personal.

"What does this remind you of?" she asked.

And the images came, uninvited. Other moments in my life where a man's voice carried the same dismissive weight, the same unspoken message: *You are here on my terms.*

I told her I felt pulled between two parts of myself: the therapist who could intellectually understand his need to control, and the woman who, outside this context, would have walked away long before. It is a strange dissonance; holding both understanding and aversion in the same breath.

We spoke about endings. That sometimes ending is the most boundaried and compassionate choice. That it can leave a residue of *what if*, even when you know it was the right call. That supervision helps you close the door without dragging guilt into the next session.

She reminded me this wasn't only a client dynamic. It was a collision of worlds: my professional ethics meeting his ideology. And sometimes, those worlds are not compatible.

By the time I left, the air felt lighter. The knot in my chest had loosened.

Supervision doesn't erase the experience, but it metabolises it. It turns raw encounter into something integrated, placed back on the shelf in my mind where it belongs.

This is the part no one sees; the quiet work behind closed doors that allows us to step back into the therapy room, ready to hold someone else's truth, without losing our own.

VII

Harry

30

The Polished Stranger

"I suppose I should just come out with it… I gamble. Not the odd flutter, more… it's my thing. My vice. Some people drink, some take drugs… me, I play. Cards, roulette, even online blackjack if it's 3 a.m. and I can't sleep."

"You're saying it's more than occasional, it's something that feels… bigger than you?"

"Bigger than me, yes. And yet, I'm very good at hiding it. You'd never guess. I'm always in control, at least, that's what I let people think. I dress well, I'm on time, I make sure bills are paid… well, most bills." He smiled, easy and disarming.

"What brings you here now?"

"The numbers are getting… ridiculous. And my wife, she doesn't know the half of it, but she's starting to suspect. I'm good at covering my tracks, but lately I've been… sloppy. Careless. I'm not used to that. I pride myself on being… composed."

"What happens when you're gambling?"

"It's like a switch flips. Everything sharpens. Colours, sounds, the rush in my chest. It's not about the money, I mean, yes, it's about the money, but it's also about the power of winning. That feeling that I can beat the odds because I'm smarter than the average man at that table."

"And when you lose?"

"I… don't lose. Not really. I just take a temporary setback." He leaned back, smiling again, as if we were sharing an inside joke. "You'll see, I always come back."

There was a kind of magnetic charm in his delivery. His voice warm, his posture open. He complimented the framed print behind me, asked how long I'd been in this space. It was flattering, and it took me a moment to notice that I was almost enjoying it. What was going on here? I made a mental note.

Over the weeks, he became a familiar presence. Always perfectly put together, cufflinks, pressed shirts, a faint trace of expensive aftershave. He told stories like a seasoned performer: tales of high-stakes poker nights, near-misses at the roulette table, a windfall that paid for a last-minute holiday to the Amalfi Coast. Tall, with a light tan, perfect hair and a charming smile. Full of confidence, jeans that were neither too tight nor too loose, a perfectly-ironed shirt in various shades of blue, and manicured hands. He had the charm of a young George Clooney and the cheek of Robbie Williams. A husband and father of two, with a successful career in Marketing in various FMCGs he name-dropped without fail.

But the closer we came to the question of why he needed the game, the more restless he became. His gambling was framed not as a compulsion, but as a skill, a talent, a mark of superiority. There was an edge of something colder beneath the charm, a calculation, a need to position himself above.

In supervision, I admitted it: I had been charmed. His politeness, his humour, even his looks, had momentarily clouded my clinical lens. My supervisor reminded me that narcissism often arrives wrapped in silk: smooth, polished, resistant to deeper exploration.

When I began gently naming patterns — the way he skirted around vulnerability, the moments he deflected with humour, I felt the shift. He became less forthcoming, more defensive.

And then, the final week, I asked a direct question:

"What would it mean for you if someone saw through the polished image?"

He smiled, but it didn't reach his eyes.

"That won't happen," he said.

The following session, he didn't turn up. No message. No call. No reply to the invoice. The polished stranger had disappeared, taking the game with him.

31

The Disappearing Act

I brought him into supervision like you bring in an object you're not sure whether to admire or handle with gloves. I described his immaculate appearance, the warmth in his voice, the compliments, the way the air shifted when he entered the room. How my own attention sharpened in his presence, as if I'd been invited into some exclusive club. I told my supervisor about the stories, glittering accounts of near-wins and grand escapes, the effortless charm.

And then I confessed the part I was less proud of: I had liked it. I had been charmed.

My supervisor didn't flinch. "It's good you noticed that," she said. "Attraction isn't the problem, it's when we don't notice it, when we let it work in the shadows."

We explored how narcissists often arrive dressed for the part, offering you a version of themselves that's all polish and precision, with just enough vulnerability to make you lean forward. But that vulnerability is often borrowed, a prop, not a truth. The real work begins when you ask for the substance underneath, when you try to open the polished box.

I told her how I had begun to sense the box was empty, or at least full of things he didn't want to show me. How, the moment I suggested that the image might be a defence, he had gone still.

"And what happened next?" she asked.

"He vanished," I said. "No message. No payment. Just gone."

She smiled, but not unkindly. "And that, too, is part of the pattern. When you risk seeing the truth, they risk losing the illusion. And for some, the illusion is worth more than the therapy."

We sat for a moment, letting the words settle.

It's an odd kind of grief, the loss of a client who was never truly present. You miss the performance, the sparkle, the promise of connection, but you know that what you were missing was never really yours to have.

Still, the room felt quieter without him.

32

Reflection: The Ones Who Leave Before They're Seen

He reminded me that not all disappearances are abrupt. Some begin the moment you ask the wrong question, wrong not because it lacks merit, but because it grazes the truth they've built their life to protect.

He taught me, too, that charm isn't warmth. It's a spotlight, warm on the outside, blinding if you stare too long. I was flattered to stand in its glow, and part of me was tempted to stay there, pretending it was enough.

But therapy isn't a stage. And I'm not the audience.

When I turned the lights toward him, he left the theatre.

I remind myself: their leaving is not my failure. Sometimes the leaving is the work, an unconscious act of self-preservation, or a rehearsed escape. Sometimes it's a performance they've perfected, so no one has to watch them drop the mask. And sometimes, it's just easier to vanish than to be seen.

Narcissistic Personality Disorder (DSM-5)

The term narcissism is often used loosely, especially on social media. Narcissistic Personality Disorder (NPD) remains a controversial DSM-5 diagnosis due to concerns over whether its criteria capture the condition without unfairly moralising or stigmatising it. The disorder is marked by persistent grandiosity, need for admiration, and preference for associating with powerful or special people, with severity ranging widely.

Research suggests three main subtypes:

1. **Grandiose/Overt Type** – High severity, poor functioning, high comorbidity (other personality disorders, substance abuse). Often angry and hostile, less likely to seek treatment. Severe cases may be "malignant narcissists" with antisocial and sadistic traits.
2. **Fragile/Vulnerable/Covert Type** – More likely to seek mental health help, often comorbid with depression and/or anxiety, highly sensitive to criticism, fluctuating self-esteem. May lack obvious grandiosity but still hold covert entitlement.
3. **High-Functioning/Exhibitionist Type** – Outwardly successful with relatively stable functioning, but still entitled and self-centred. May only meet NPD criteria during crises, often better described as having narcissistic traits.

Boundaries between subtypes blur, and extreme cases, such as historical dictators, highlight the potential societal harm of malignant narcissism. However, many individuals with NPD experience genuine psychological suffering, often rooted in early trauma or neglect, and can benefit from treatment focused on self-awareness and empathy.

Ongoing research into subtypes may improve diagnosis,

reduce stigma, and guide better treatment approaches.

VIII

Fiyori

33

Against All … Gods

Because of my own background — or at least that's how I explain it — I seem to attract clients from many cultures, ethnicities, and mixed heritages. Over the years I've worked with people from every corner of the world, and what still fascinates me is how much unites us despite the distance or the time zones. Occasionally, though, beliefs collide.

As therapists we are taught to practise *unconditional positive regard,* a term coined by Carl Rogers, one of the fathers of modern psychology. It means offering complete acceptance of the person in front of us, without conditions or judgement. Accepting someone for who they are: thoughts, feelings, and all, without needing them to change.

Fiyori was a young woman from Ethiopia. Her name, she explained, meant "Flower." She was a maternal health advocate, a singer, strikingly beautiful, and she lived in London while her estranged husband remained in Ethiopia. She travelled constantly, juggling work and three young children.

That day she came in with a familiar brightness in her eyes, the one I'd learned to recognise. The light that meant she had seen something.

"I had another dream," she said before even removing her coat. She perched on the edge of the sofa, eager, certain.

"In the dream, I was standing on a cliff, and the wind was so strong I thought it would push me over. But then He was there. He told me to go ahead with the move. He said He would provide. I woke up and I knew. I don't have to worry anymore."

Her hands fluttered as she spoke, palms opening as if in offering. Her conviction was almost tangible.

"I hear how much certainty this gave you," I said.

"Yes," she breathed. "Because it was Him. I know His voice. And this morning I saw a dove in the garden. That's a sign. I've been praying for guidance and He's showing me the way."

Inside, my own voice questioned: *What if it's not a sign? What if it's just a dove? What if you're handing over the wheel to something that lives only in your mind?*

I reminded myself: my work is not to argue with her God, but to explore what her God means in her life, and what happens when she acts on that belief.

"And if the signs led you somewhere you didn't expect?" I asked.

She looked at me, startled. "But they wouldn't. God wouldn't do that."

There it was: the wall. Not of anger, but of certainty.

I felt the tension in my own chest; and a respect for her faith held alongside unease about the power it had over her choices.

Not to dismantle her belief, but to create a space where belief could meet curiosity. Where signs could be held to the light, not to disprove them, but to understand their place in her life.

She smiled. "I think you understand," she said.

And in a way, I did. Just not in the way she thought.

34

Reflection: Between Belief and Question

I am not here to save souls; I am here to hear them. But sometimes a client's faith walks into the room before they do, tall and unwavering, filling the space so completely that my own presence feels small in comparison.

I admire conviction. I admire the comfort it gives, the way her eyes soften when she speaks of her God, the certainty she carries in a world where most people stumble through fog. When Geoff was in the hospice, I saw how faith, any faith, gave people solace. While I tried to make sense through psychology and neuroscience, they found it through prayer. Guess who won.

So yes, I admire her certainty. And yet I fear it too. I fear what happens when dreams become directives, when signs are followed without question, when a dove on a balcony becomes a command. Certainty without space for doubt risks sliding into dogma.

My work demands I meet her where she is, even if it's at the edge of a cliff in her dream. It demands I neither push her down nor pull her away, but that I stand beside her and ask: *What if the wind blew the other way?*

This is the part of the job people don't write about: holding two truths at once, the client's faith and your own doubts, without crushing either.

Faith, I remind myself, is a landscape. My role is not to change the terrain, but to walk it with her long enough that she can see all of it — flowers and cliffs, sunlight and shadow.

And maybe that's enough. Maybe walking beside someone is holy work in its own right.

35

When the Signs Demand Action

She was calmer this time, no rush in her step, but there was determination in her eyes, as though her bags were already packed in her mind.

"I've decided," she said, settling into the sofa.

"I'm quitting my job. God told me it's time to step into my calling. I had another dream: I was walking through a field of wheat and the path opened up before me. And then yesterday, my phone battery died at 4:44 p.m. That's a sign."

Her words were steady, as if a sequence of numbers and a vision were as factual as a payslip.

"Leaving your job is a big decision," I said carefully.

"Yes, but it's right. The signs are clear."

Inside, the alarm was steady: *What if this isn't guidance but impulse wrapped in holiness?*

"And what does stepping into your calling look like?" I asked.

She smiled faintly. "I don't know yet. That's the faith part. He'll show me."

I wanted to anchor her, but instead I asked: "How will you manage your finances in the meantime?"

She tilted her head, almost amused. "You really don't understand faith, do you?"

The truth was, I understood it too well. I knew how intoxicating it felt to believe you were chosen, guided, protected. And how dangerous it could be when conviction stood in place of a plan.

We circled each other for the rest of the hour: her faith, my questions, her certainty, my unease. Neither of us moved the other. That wasn't the point. The point was to hold the conversation open long enough for her to see that faith and practicality do not have to cancel each other out.

As she left, she said, "You'll see. God has this all figured out."

I watched her go, respect and worry mixing in my chest. Faith is easy to admire when it doesn't demand sacrifice. It is harder when the altar is built from rent money.

I reminded myself: I am not her parent, her employer, or her God. I am her therapist. My work is not to forbid, but to invite reflection. Not to dismantle her belief, but to test its foundations before she builds her house on it.

Respect is not silence. Challenge is not disrespect. The art is knowing when to lean into each.

36

After the Leap

It had been six weeks since I'd last seen her. No message. No cancellation. Just absence. Then, on a wet Thursday afternoon, she walked back in.

The smile was still there, but smaller now, like a flower battered by rain.

"I did it," she said. "I left."

"At first, it was amazing. I felt light, free. I was waking up without an alarm clock, reading my Bible in the mornings, walking in the park. I thought, this is what He wanted for me."

Her voice faltered. "But… I haven't found the next step yet. I've sent applications, but nothing's come through. And the rent…" She trailed off.

I felt the ache before I spoke. "Tell me about the signs now."

"I still see them. Yesterday, a dove landed on my balcony railing. That has to mean something, right?"

It wasn't mine to answer. My role wasn't to confirm or deny her signs, but to explore what they meant in the context of her reality.

"What does it mean to you?" I asked.

"That I shouldn't give up. That I need to keep trusting. But part of me wonders if I misheard Him. Or if I'm failing some test."

There it was… the crack in certainty. Not wide enough to collapse her faith, but wide enough for doubt to breathe.

"What would it be like if the signs were one part of your decision-making, and not the only part?" I asked.

She looked at me for a long time. "I don't know. Maybe safer. But then… would it still be faith?"

We sat in silence, the kind that marks the beginning of a shift, one that may take months or years to complete.

When she left, I realised something: faith and reality aren't enemies, but they don't always speak the same language. My job isn't to translate one into the other. It's to help her develop more than one dialect to call her own.

IX

Sarah

37

Beware of Greeks Bearing Gifts

You might wonder what the problem is if, at the end of therapy, you give your therapist a thank you card and some flowers. That might be fine. Even Freud, who explicitly warned against gift exchange, often accepted presents from his patients during treatment.

The phrase *Beware of Greeks bearing gifts* comes from Ancient Greece. It was a warning against accepting offerings from enemies or from those with hidden motives. It originated with the story of the Trojan Horse in Virgil's *Aeneid*, where the Greeks presented a giant wooden horse to the Trojans. Believed to be a gift, it was in fact filled with soldiers who later attacked the city.

Sarah was in her mid-forties, a senior executive in pharmaceuticals, flying so often that the glamour had worn thin. She could recite cabin crew instructions word for word: "Doors armed and cross-checked… in the unlikely event of loss of oxygen… put on your own mask before helping others." In her life, though, she put her own mask on last — or not at all. Burned out, overworked, under-loved.

One morning she arrived carrying two tall paper cups, the green mermaid logo visible from the doorway.

"I thought you might like a coffee," she said, placing one on the table before sitting down.

It seemed casual, but I felt a flicker of surprise. We had been working for months on her paruresis, a condition that turned public toilets into battlegrounds. Control was always at the centre of our conversations: what she could control, what she couldn't, and what she feared losing.

The heat seeped through the cup into my hands as we began, her update familiar — mapping outings by toilet availability, the exhaustion of constant planning. Yet the coffee sat between us, quietly altering the space.

Only later, after the cup was empty, did the thought take root. What did it mean? She had been late more often recently, always with an excuse, yet she still found time to buy coffee.

Gifts in therapy are rarely just gifts. They are acts, messages, sometimes negotiations. A coffee can be gratitude, an offering, a reversal of roles: the client taking care of the therapist.

The next week, she arrived with another. Same brand, same deliberate placing on the table, five minutes late again.

"I noticed you've brought me coffee the last two sessions," I said. "I'm curious what it means for you."

She looked surprised, then laughed. "I guess it's nice to feel like I'm giving something back. You always listen. I thought maybe I could do something for you."

Her words were simple, but the meaning ran deeper. In a life where she often felt exposed, where even her body betrayed her, the coffee was competence. Proof she could give, not just receive.

We spoke about that. About how it felt to give in this space, about her guilt for "just talking" each week. As though her presence alone was not enough.

The truth was, the coffee wasn't for me. It was for her. A token of capability, a sign she could provide for someone else, however small.

The following week she came in empty-handed.

"I thought about bringing coffee," she said, "but I decided just to be here instead. That's okay, right?"

"Yes," I replied. "It's more than okay."

And it was.

38

When a Coffee is More Than a Coffee

In therapy, gifts arrive with invisible strings. Not obligations, but threads connecting to something deeper in the giver's world. They are never just gifts.

A coffee, a box of chocolates, a plant; each carries layers of meaning. Sometimes gratitude, sometimes an attempt to rebalance the inequality of the therapeutic relationship, sometimes a bid for closeness or to test boundaries.

In psychodynamic work, the act of giving is rarely neutral. It expresses something, often a negotiation.

For this client, the coffee was not caffeine. It was agency in a life where control was fragile. It was a reversal; for once, she was the provider. Perhaps, unconsciously, it was also a way to bridge the gap between us, to make the space less clinical, more equal. A chance to prove she had something of value to give beyond her story.

As coffee is a diuretic, it may even have carried another layer of meaning. She could only drink it in a safe place.

The challenge as a therapist is to walk the line between appreciation and curiosity. Accepting without question risks missing the meaning. Refusing outright risks shame or rupture. Instead, we name it. We explore it. We hold it up to the light.

Because in therapy, a coffee is never just a coffee.

It wasn't the first gift I'd received. One client brought baklava each Christmas, still warm, wrapped in foil. She said she "had too much at home," but it was clear it was her way of offering me a piece of herself, her culture, her care.

Another, a young man, left a brand new book on the chair after a session. He didn't say it was for me. I only found it later. The book was about parents. Perhaps the closest he could come to saying: *I wish I'd had one like you.*

Another client brought a plant, then returned anxiously two weeks later to ask if it was still alive. The plant was a test. If I had cared for it, perhaps I could care for her too. If it had died, perhaps she was right that she was "too much."

In every case, the object was never just an object.

A biscuit was a bridge. A book was a confession. A plant was a question.

Over the years I've come to see gifts in four broad ways. Sometimes they are a defence, a way to hide anger, dependency, or shame. Sometimes they are about the relationship, a reflection of how the client once related to parents, partners, or authority figures. Sometimes they reveal deeper patterns of attachment. And sometimes they are simply gratitude, a sign of growth.

At their simplest, gifts are a window into how a person experiences giving and receiving. What they choose, how they offer it, what they hope will follow — all of it tells their story.

General Note on Transference

The concept of transference is central in psychotherapy. It

involves the unconscious redirection of a client's feelings and expectations from past relationships onto the therapist, often providing valuable insight into their inner world (Hayes et al., 2018).

X

Eleanor

39

The Symbiosis

Eleanor was in her fifties but looked closer to forty, partly through DNA and partly because she looked after herself. Well established in the legal industry, she had climbed the corporate ladder and was now a partner in one of the Big 5 Consulting firms. She did everything hard: worked hard, played hard, gave her blood, sweat and tears to her career. Single by choice, no children, no strings, though she admitted to occasional partners along the way.

That Wednesday, she sat across from me, posture perfect, hands folded in her lap, like someone who had learned long ago how to hold herself together.

"My mother… she just couldn't cope. Even when I was little, I knew she wasn't really there. Anxious about everything, panicking over nothing, retreating into her room. And then there was my sister, younger, fragile. Someone had to hold it all together. So, I did."

Her voice was calm, matter-of-fact, but the weight was unmistakable.

"It sounds like, very early on, you felt you had to step into the role of the parent."

She answered instantly. "Yes. I didn't even think about it. I just took over. Made sure my sister got to school, calmed Mum down when she had episodes, cooked dinners. I was eight years old. No one asked me. I just knew, if I didn't, nothing would work."

In Transactional Analysis terms, this is called a *symbiosis*: the child unconsciously steps into the adult role and sacrifices their own needs to keep the family afloat.

"You had to grow up very fast. To be the adult when you should have been the child."

Her eyes welled. "Yes. And the thing is, people praised me for it. Teachers said I was mature. Relatives said I was responsible. Even my mother thanked me. It became who I was."

"And inside?" I asked.

"I don't even know what I want. I only know what others need."

Silence held for a moment.

"What would it be like if, in here, you didn't have to hold it all together? If you could allow yourself to be cared for?"

Her lips trembled. "Scary. But maybe freeing."

Note on Symbiosis

The term *symbiosis* comes from the Greek words *sym* ("together") and *bios* ("life"), and in biology it describes a close, long-term interaction between two organisms. In psychology, the concept is used to explain relational patterns where one person unconsciously takes on roles that compensate for what the other cannot provide. This can range from healthy (such as temporary dependency after surgery, where the nurse provides support until recovery) to unhealthy (such as a couple where one always decides and the other passively follows). Transactional Analysis theory suggests that every symbiosis is an attempt to meet developmental needs that were left unmet in childhood, often replaying past dynamics in the hope of resolving them in adult life (Stewart & Joines, 2002, p. 217).

40

Naming the Pattern and Giving the Child a Voice

The following week she came in lighter. "I thought about what you said... about not having to hold it all together. It stayed with me. I realised I don't even know what that feels like."

We named what had happened: she had stepped into her mother's role, becoming the Parent when her Child still needed care.

"So part of me was doing my mum's job?" she asked.

"Exactly. You became the Parent and even the Adult. But your Child had no space."

Her eyes glistened. "I don't even know what my Child would want now."

"That's the work we can do. Giving her a voice."

The next week she came in hesitant, almost shy. "I tried something. I let myself buy a silly magazine, the kind with puzzles and celebrity gossip. It felt childish. But part of me was happy."

"That sounds like your Child wanting something just for fun."

She laughed quietly. “It was fun. And then I thought, is this allowed? Am I allowed to just… enjoy something?”

“Yes,” I said. “That’s exactly what your Child has been waiting for.”

41

Resistance and a New Decision

Her tone shifted again the following session. "I feel guilty. Like I'm betraying my mother by not always putting others first. She needed me, and I stepped up. Isn't that what a good daughter does?"

"That's the Parent voice still echoing," I said. "It kept you safe once, but maybe it doesn't have to define you now."

She frowned, considering it. "So… I can reframe it?"

"Yes. You can make a new decision."

The week after, she arrived with a small slip of paper. Her handwriting was neat but trembling.

"I wrote it down: *I don't have to play that role anymore. I can be the Adult I am today. I can let my Child have needs and joy.*"

Her eyes softened with relief. "For the first time, I feel like my life could belong to me."

42

Testing the Boundaries

Not long after, she arrived conflicted. "My sister called, asking for money again. Normally, I'd just pay it. But this time I paused… and I said no."

"That's your new decision in action," I said.

Her lips tightened. "Yes, but then I cried for an hour. I felt cruel, like I'd abandoned her. My mother's voice echoed in my head: Don't be selfish. Family comes first."

I reassured her. "The guilt doesn't mean you did the wrong thing. It means you're stepping into new ground. Guilt is often the shadow of change."

Later, her sister lashed out. "She said I was heartless, that I've changed. And I started to wonder if she's right. Maybe I am becoming cold."

"It sounds like she's reacting to losing the Parent you always were for her. That doesn't make you cold. It means you're no longer carrying what was never yours to carry."

She wiped tears. "But if I'm not the responsible one, who am I?"

"That's the work ahead. To discover who you are outside of

that role."

43

Reclaiming Play and Integration

One day she walked in carrying a small sketchpad. "I used to love drawing as a girl, but I told myself it was a waste of time. Last night, I drew for an hour. Just for me."

Her eyes shone with pride.

"That's your Child finding a voice again," I said.

She smiled. "It felt innocent. Like she's still there. I forgot she even existed."

Weeks later, she spoke with a new steadiness.

"I'm starting to see it differently. Saying no doesn't make me selfish. It makes me honest. My Adult can choose when I give, instead of being forced to."

"That's a profound shift," I said.

She leaned forward, voice firm. "And I realised something: my Child doesn't just need play. She needs protecting. She needs my Adult to stand up for her."

Her face softened. "For the first time, I feel like I could be whole."

XI

Mark

44

Parallel Lives

Mark was an engineer in his late forties, married to a lawyer, with two grown-up children, one already out of the house. Our sessions were slow, heavy with silences, marked by long pauses and wordless gestures.

That day, he sank into the chair and stared at the floor.

"I don't even know why I came today. Nothing's wrong, exactly. But nothing's right either."

"Nothing's wrong and nothing's right," I repeated. "Sounds like you're in between."

He gave a hollow laugh. "In between what? Life? Death? I wake up, go to work, come home, eat dinner, sit next to my wife, watch telly, and then it's the same again the next day. On repeat. I'm a machine that doesn't even know what it's making anymore."

"How does it feel, saying that out loud?"

He rubbed his hands together, avoiding my gaze. "Strange. Shameful, really. Like I'm admitting defeat. Men aren't supposed to say this. We're meant to just get on with it."

"According to whom?"

He shrugged. "Everyone. I've done it for years. But lately… I can't keep up the act."

When I asked what he wanted instead, he shook his head. "I don't know."

"What's it like sitting next to your wife?"

"She's… there. Reliable. Predictable. We don't argue, but we don't connect either. It's like we live parallel lives. Side by side but never touching. And sometimes I think, is this it? Wake up, work, dinner, sleep, until I die?"

The words hung in the air, heavy and resigned. His eyes glistened, though he quickly looked away.

Later, he spoke again. "Dinner is silent. Sometimes she mentions the neighbour, her book club, the weather. I nod. She nods. Then it's over."

"What's it like to sit in that silence with her?"

"Agonising. And safe, at the same time. If we don't talk, nothing explodes. Nothing changes. It's peaceful, but dead. Like living in a museum. Everything's neat, in its place, but there's no life."

He pressed his palms into his thighs as if bracing himself. "I look at her and think, we're strangers. And then I think, maybe that's my fault. Maybe I stopped trying years ago. Maybe I don't know how."

Silence settled again, thick and impenetrable. He blamed himself, yet feared the truth. If he asked her whether she felt the same, he risked confirming either that the emptiness was his alone, or that they had both wasted thirty years. For him, both outcomes felt unbearable.

I reminded him that he had still chosen to come here. He let out a faint laugh. "Maybe that was a mistake."

"Or maybe it was something else," I said.

"Like what?"

"Like a part of you not wanting to just exist."

He exhaled, whispering, "Maybe. It's all I've got."

It was barely audible, but that "maybe" mattered.

45

A Glimpse of Longing

One session, his voice cracked as he described a dream. "We were young again, me and her. Laughing, running through a field. She touched my hand. Just touched it. And it felt electric, like something I haven't felt in years."

"You still remember the feeling."

He nodded slowly. "I woke up aching. Not just sad, aching. Because I realised how much I miss her. Not her exactly. The us that used to exist."

"You're grieving that us."

"Yeah. And I don't know if it's dead forever, or if it's buried under all these years. But the dream… it reminded me that once, it was alive."

The longing pained him, yet it revealed something vital: a capacity to want. For a man who had started with "nothing's wrong, nothing's right," this was the first sign of life.

46

The Slow Return

Weeks later, he entered with a different sigh — not despair, but weariness edged with relief.

"I've been thinking about that dream. About holding her hand. I keep replaying it, like I don't want to lose it."

"What does it mean that you're holding onto it?"

"That maybe I'm not done. Maybe we're not done. For so long I thought we were just waiting to die, side by side. But maybe we're waiting for something else."

He described asking his wife to walk with him. She agreed. Nothing dramatic was said, but they walked in quiet comfort.

"It reminded me she was once the person I wanted to tell everything to. Maybe she still could be."

When I asked how he felt about himself in that moment, his voice softened. "Less invisible. Less pointless. Like if she can still want to walk with me, maybe I matter after all."

The fog hadn't lifted completely, but breaks in the clouds had begun to appear. Change came not through grand declarations, but through the ordinary — a hand across a table, a walk around the block.

For Mark, therapy wasn't about fixing his marriage or erasing his despair. It was about rediscovering that "maybe." Depression had told him he was finished. He had begun to whisper back: not yet.

XII

The Frame of Therapy

47

The Ones Who Don't Pay

They never tell you, in training, how much you'll have to think about money.

Not in the obvious ways, not about fees, or the length of sessions, or whether you can afford a new chair for your practice. I mean the money that doesn't arrive. The session that gets quieter not because the client has run out of words, but because they've stopped paying for the space altogether.

Receiving no bank transfer after a session where you've held someone through their panic, their childhood trauma, their fractured morning is more common than you might think. The absence of that simple transaction becomes oddly loud. You refresh your account. Nothing. A day passes. Two. Then you send the gentle reminder: *I haven't been able to find your payment for this week's session, could you please help me?*

Some reply. Others don't. And the silence starts to speak.

You wouldn't go to Tesco, pick up a can of Coke, and expect the cashier to remind you later that payment is outstanding. So why does it happen in therapy?

Of course, this isn't just about money.

For some clients, the missed payment is a scream disguised as a shrug. A way to say: *You don't get to tell me what to do.* Or: *Let's see if you'll still care about me if I break the rules.* Others are ashamed, not of the invoice, but of needing help in the first place. For them, paying means admitting they're receiving care. They don't believe they deserve it, or they don't want to feel weak. Paying becomes proof that something is wrong with them.

And then there are those whose delays are not about resistance, but repetition. Old ghosts showing up through the calendar. Parents who were never consistent, teachers who forgot their name, systems that ignored their voice. To pay on time would be to act differently, to break the pattern. That kind of healing takes time.

One client, early forties, would pay only when prompted, every single week. Her anxiety was sky-high. Her guilt even higher. Each reminder was met with frantic apologies and explanations about her schedule, her banking application, her memory. But in session, she was brilliant. Insightful and engaged. We were doing deep work.

And yet... the payment never arrived on its own.

It wasn't forgetfulness. It was part of the therapy. Her unconscious resistance showed up as a notification delay, and addressing it, naming it, became the work. *What does it mean that you forget to pay me? How do you feel about the fact that I have to remind you?* Those questions cracked something open. We didn't talk about money. We talked about worth.

But then there are those who simply stop. They cancel a session last minute. They vanish mid-block. No email. No closure. The absence is sharp, not just of payment, but of presence.

And you're left wondering: Did they hate it? Did I miss something? Did they lose faith in me? In therapy? In themselves? The mind spins. The balance tilts. And still, you're supposed to hold the boundary, professionally, ethically, quietly.

No one prepares you for the emotional gymnastics of keeping compassion alive while enforcing a payment policy. Of interpreting resistance without becoming resentful. Of knowing when to explore the meaning behind the avoidance, and when to simply say: *This is the agreement. We either honour it, or we pause the work.*

Because that's the truth. Therapy is not a favour. It's not a luxury. It's a relationship, and payment is part of the frame that holds it together. Without that, it begins to collapse under its own emotional weight.

So, there's a chapter in every therapist's career titled *The Ones Who Don't Pay.* But the story is never really about the money. It's about grief, control, shame, testing, re-enactment. It's about clients saying, through their absence: *Are you still there? Are you angry with me? Will you leave me like the others?*

And it's about us, the therapists, sitting in that uncertain space with open hands and firm boundaries, holding both their fear and our own frustration, and knowing that sometimes the work lives in the places where the invoice never comes.

XIII

Boundaries in Practice

48

The Edges of the Hour

Time in therapy is never just time. It is part of the frame, the structure that makes the work possible. Fifty minutes. Sixty minutes. Whatever the agreed container is, it holds the session like a bowl holds water. Without the edges, everything spills out.

Clients rarely think about it this way. To them, the hour is elastic, expanding when they need more, shrinking when they dread being here. For me, the edges matter. They signal safety. They give us both the certainty that there is a beginning and an end, that this is a protected space.

Most doorknob comments are not emergencies. They are unconscious offerings, important truths slipped in casually at the very edge of the session, when the clock is ticking and the words almost feel safer because there's no time left to unpack them. That's what makes them fascinating. They challenge the frame and test the boundaries, arriving right when I say, *"We'll have to stop for today."*

And yet, endings in therapy are rarely neat. There is something therapists call the *doorknob moment,* when the most charged material surfaces in the last two minutes of the session, as the client reaches for their coat or the Zoom clock ticks down. *"By the way,"* they say casually, *"I think I don't want to live anymore."* Or, *"I never told anyone this, but..."* It's not manipulation. It's often fear, or hope, a longing to leave something heavy in my hands as they walk out, to keep the connection alive between now and next time.

And then there are the messages. A WhatsApp ping after 11 p.m., a long email between sessions. Sometimes it's practical, a cancellation, a payment. Sometimes it's raw: *"I can't stop crying,"* or *"Do you think I'm crazy?"* These moments test the frame. Do I respond now, or hold the boundary and wait? If I reply instantly, I risk becoming an on-call lifeline rather than a therapist. If I don't, I risk them feeling abandoned.

The truth is, holding time is about more than calendars and clocks. It's about containment. When a client knows the session ends at 4:00 p.m., and that I will not answer their 11:00 p.m. text, it's not cruelty. It's structure. It's the invisible scaffolding that allows us to do the real work safely, predictably.

Sometimes, I wonder how much of therapy is simply this: two humans agreeing on a beginning and an end, and what can unfold in between. The middle may be messy, but the frame is solid. And in a world where everything feels porous, that solidity is rare and sacred.

Common Doorknob Comments

The Therapy Itself

- *"I'm not sure this therapy is right for me. I've booked with someone new."*

- *"Oh, I won't be here for three weeks, business trip. See you in May."*
- *"By the way, today's my last session. Thank you for everything."*

Big Life Changes

- *"I don't know why I didn't tell you earlier, but I've decided to sell everything and move to Costa Rica. Do you think I should?"*
- *"I quit my job yesterday... actually, I got fired. I wasn't sure I wanted to talk about it."*

Mental Health Bombshells

- *"I've been feeling suicidal again. Didn't want you to worry."*
- *"I think I might be a narcissist. Am I?"*
- *"I'm drinking a lot more. I think it's out of control."*

Family Surprises

- *"Have a nice holiday! I'll be with my family, haven't seen them in twenty years."*
- *"Turns out I have a half-sibling. Have a good week!"*

Curiosity About Me

- *"So, where are you going on holiday?"*
- *"I saw you at that bar last week, nice moves!"*
- *"What were you looking for at the pharmacy?"*

Doorknob comments aren't random. They often point to something that feels too hot to handle in the middle of the session. Some of the unconscious dynamics include:

- **Not Enough Time:** Sometimes there isn't room to explore everything, especially if we meet infrequently. More often, it's about what the ending represents — loss, separation, abandonment. The pressure of goodbye stirs up old feelings, and something slips out.
- **Early Days:** When the relationship is new, trust is still forming. Saying the hard thing right before leaving can feel safer.
- **Avoidance:** Shame, fear, social anxiety — these can make direct disclosure hard, so the words sneak out at the last second.
- **Defences:** Some clients habitually leave things until the eleventh hour, a learned way of controlling closeness or avoiding discomfort.
- **Testing:** Bringing something big at the end is often a way to see how I respond: *Will you stay calm? Will the frame hold?* It's a test of safety, and in its own way, an act of trust.
- **Countertransference[1]:** Sometimes it's about me. If I appear rushed or uneasy, clients pick it up. Doorknob comments can be a mirror of the relational dynamic.

The Therapist's Split-Second Decision

When it happens, I have seconds to decide: do we stop on time, extend, or schedule an extra session? If it's a genuine crisis, I'll ensure the client leaves safe, even if that means bending the frame. Most of the time, though, I don't dive in. I name it:

"I hear how important that sounds. We can hold it here and start with it next time."

It can feel harsh in the moment, yet it's therapeutic, because the frame holds even when the feelings are big. And that consistency, more than anything, builds trust.

The Value of Doorknob Moments

Over time, clients learn to notice these impulses and bring them in sooner. That's growth: becoming aware of what lingers at the edge of consciousness and finding the courage to name it while there's still space to explore.

Doorknob moments are not inconveniences. They're raw material. They show us where the heat is, where the longing hides, where the fear whispers. They remind us that therapy is rarely linear, and that even small endings, such as the close of an hour, stir something deep.

When managed well, these moments don't just close a session. They open a door.

[1] ***Countertransference*** refers to the therapist's unconscious emotional responses to the client, shaped by their own history and internal world. Originally a psychoanalytic concept (Freud, 1910), it has since been recognised across therapeutic approaches as an important tool for understanding the relational dynamics in the room.

Epilogue

Looking back over these sessions, the stories, the silences, the ruptures, and the small movements of change, I'm struck by how therapy is never just about fixing a problem. It is about sitting with another human being in their rawest form and holding what they cannot yet carry themselves. It is about surviving the helplessness when someone vanishes mid-process, or when a door closes before the work is done. It is about staying steady when gifts arrive, when anger erupts, when idealisation clouds the air. It is about being human, and at the same time, being something more: a witness, a container, a mirror.

Each client takes me somewhere different. Into grief that refuses tidy stages. Into faith and visions of God that stretch my own sense of belief. Into addictions and resistances that flare brightly, then slip into the dark when truth presses too close. Into childhood contracts where a daughter becomes a parent before she learns to play. Into transference that seduces, enrages, abandons, or clings. Into the fragile choreography of money, payment, and worth.

I once thought the therapist's role was to illuminate, to lead people out of the dark. Now I know it is something quieter. It is about keeping a flame alive, so that when they are ready, they can see by their own light.

Some stories end abruptly, unfinished. Others stretch over years and change us both in ways neither could have predicted.

Always, the work remains open, because human lives are open.

I carry these encounters with me. They sit beneath the surface when I meet someone new, shaping how I listen, how I pause, how I breathe. They remind me that therapy is not a science of perfection but an art of presence. That the value lies not in the brilliance of interpretation, but in the courage to stay. To witness. To remain open.

And when the room empties, when the last word fades into silence, what remains is this truth: healing is never neat, never finished, but it is always possible. And sometimes, that is enough.

Bibliography & Further Reading

1. Berne, Eric. *Principles of Group Treatment*. Shea Books, 1966.
2. Boliston Mardula, J. "Appetite Path Model: Working with Escape Hatch Resolution with Clients who Use Drugs and Alcohol." *TA UK*, vol. 61, Autumn 2001, pp. 9–14.
3. Brown, C., and H. B. Trangsrud. "Factors Associated with Acceptance and Decline of Client Gift Giving." *Professional Psychology: Research and Practice*, vol. 39, no. 5, 2008, pp. 505–511. doi:10.1037/0735-7028.39.5.505.
4. Caligor, E., K. N. Levy, and F. E. Yeomans. "Narcissistic Personality Disorder: Diagnostic and Clinical Challenges." *American Journal of Psychiatry*, vol. 172, 2015, pp. 415–423.
5. American Psychiatric Association. *Diagnostic and Statistical Manual of Mental Disorders (DSM-5)*. American Psychiatric Publishing, 2013.
6. Hayes, J. A., C. J. Gelso, S. Goldberg, and D. M. Kivlighan. "Countertransference Management and Effective Psychotherapy: Meta-Analytic Findings." *Psychotherapy*, vol. 55, no. 4, Dec. 2018, pp. 496–507. doi:10.1037/pst0000189.
7. Joines, Vann, and Ian Stewart. *Personality Adaptations: A New Guide to Human Understanding in Psychotherapy and Counselling*. Lifespace Publishing, 2002.

8. Perry, Matthew. *Friends, Lovers, and the Big Terrible Thing*. Headline, 2022.
9. Perry, Philippa. *Couch Fiction: A Graphic Tale of Psychotherapy*. Palgrave Macmillan, 2010.
10. Rogers, Carl R. "The Necessary and Sufficient Conditions of Therapeutic Personality Change." *Journal of Consulting Psychology*, vol. 21, no. 2, 1957, pp. 95–103.
11. Russ, E., J. Shedler, R. Bradley, and D. Westen. "Refining the Construct of Narcissistic Personality Disorder: Diagnostic Criteria and Subtypes." *American Journal of Psychiatry*, vol. 165, 2008, pp. 1473–1481.
12. Selby, C. L. B. *The Psychology of Eating Disorders*. Springer Publishing Company, 2019.
13. Smolar, A. I. "Reflections on Gifts in the Therapeutic Setting: The Gift from Patient to Therapist." *American Journal of Psychotherapy*, vol. 56, no. 1, 2002, pp. 27–45. doi:10.1176/appi.psychotherapy.2002.56.1.27.
14. Stewart, Ian, and Vann Joines. *TA Today: A New Introduction to Transactional Analysis*. Lifespace Publishing, 2012.
15. Van der Kolk, Bessel A. *The Body Keeps the Score: Brain, Mind and Body in the Treatment of Trauma*. Viking Press, 2015.
16. Werbart, A., U. Rådberg, I. Holm, D. Forsström, and A. H. Berman. "The Meaning and Feeling of the Time and Space Between Psychotherapy Sessions and Everyday Life: Client Experiences of Transitions." *Psychotherapy Research*, vol. 34, no. 7, 2023, pp. 899–912.

About the Author

As a Chartered Psychologist and Executive Coach with over 25 years of experience across HR, leadership, and organisational consulting, I set up the Leadership Psychology Institute back in 2007 to work with senior leaders who are tired of vague advice and one-size-fits-all frameworks. Most of my work starts when something's stuck; conversations aren't happening, teams are splintering, or a leader's hit a wall and no amount of motivational quotes are going to fix it.

My work includes focusing on group dynamics, trust, conflict, decision-making and motivation. I work with boards, senior teams and individual leaders to help them make the big decisions, say what needs saying, and figure out how to lead without losing their grip on what matters.

I've worked across the UK, Europe, Africa and the Middle East. Before setting up my own consultancy, I spent 14 years in senior HR roles with companies like Diageo, SCA, Henkel-Ecolab and Johnson & Johnson. I'm a Chartered Psychologist, HCPC-registered, MCC and ACTC accredited with the ICF, certified by the Kantor Institute and a Fellow of the Institute of Leadership.

Part of my time is dedicated to my Private Practice as a Psychotherapist (Sweetbriar Therapy) that was set up in 2017 supporting individuals. Psychotherapy and Counselling are mainly, though not exclusively, listening-and-talking-based methods of addressing psychological and psychosomatic issues and change, situational dilemmas, crises, developmental needs. Psychotherapy can help you discuss feelings you have about yourself and other people, particularly family and those close to you.

Typical Examples include:

Bereavement

Relationships (Family, Work, Other)

Family Breakdown / Separation / Divorce

Stress – Coping with Anxiety

Depression

Racial / Cultural Issues

Eating Disorders (Anorexia, Bulimia, Binge-Eating Disorder)

Managing / Dealing with Change

Work-related Issues (Managing your Boss, your Team, feeling excluded, etc.)

Self-Belief & Self-Esteem

... and many others

Outside of work, I run a vintage unit together with friends at a local antiques emporium where I collect and sell pieces that catch my eye. I live with Eddy, my rescue dog and partner in crime, and keep active with a bit of lifting, walking and rummaging through car boot sales at the weekend.

That's me in a nutshell! Psychologist by trade, vintage hoarder by habit, dog mum by force!

You can connect with me on:

- https://leadershippsychologyinstitute.com
- https://www.linkedin.com/in/maria-katsarou-makin

Also by Dr Maria Katsarou-Makin

Dr Maria Katsarou-Makin's work spans stress, grief, and leadership. From practical strategies to manage workplace stress, to an honest exploration of loss and the carer's role in *Factions of a Mind,* to uncovering the hidden dynamics of executive teams in *Group Dyna-Mix,* her books bring clarity to subjects often left unspoken. Together, they form a body of work that is both accessible and deeply human.

Group Dyna-Mix

Since the 2008 financial crisis, executive leadership has come under close scrutiny, exposing hidden team dynamics that are often difficult to access, challenge, or understand. Drawing on Patrick Lencioni's insights, Maria highlights how avoidance of accountability, lack of commitment, and neglect of results shape the culture of leadership teams.

In Group Dyna-Mix, Dr Katsarou-Makin examines the relationship between trust and team behaviour among executives, where unspoken codes and familial-style bonds often dictate who is included, how decisions are made, and where responsibility lies. She explores how this trust both enables and undermines performance, asking what values it demands, what actions it creates, and where it ultimately fails.

Factions of a Mind

After losing her husband within three months, Maria experienced a raw awakening to grief and its stages. She reflects on how loss reshapes character, affects those around us, and tests the role of carers who must comfort loved ones while carrying their own pain.

In *Factions of a Mind,* Dr Katsarou-Makin examines the realities of caring: the weight of responsibility, the suffering it brings, and the silence around caring for ourselves once the person we supported is gone. She explores how unpreparedness for grief leaves carers vulnerable, offering an honest account of duty, loss, and the need for self-compassion.

Under Pressure

Everyone needs some pressure to perform at work, but when pressure tips into stress it becomes harmful, counter-productive, and sometimes devastating.

Stress is often ignored in workplaces because acknowledging it is wrongly seen as weakness. This book explores the realities of modern working life, where challenges are greater than ever, and offers practical techniques to recognise and manage stress before it escalates. It provides a clear understanding of this often-misunderstood state and shows how to address it before the consequences become damaging.

Printed in Dunstable, United Kingdom

67552125R00102